The Guardians

With Clarice & Tara Grey

Book 4

Josef Peeters

Edited by: Rosemary Hillyard

Editing Services, rmhillyard@aol.com

Cover design by Rocking Book Covers,
https://www.rockingbookcovers.com

ISBN-13: 9780645028843

DEDICATION

I dedicate this book to the readers and friends who have
supported me through the series.

OTHER BOOKS BY THE AUTHOR

Fiction:
Dumped (psych drama)
Daintree Denizens (thriller)
Mt. Moulamein (sci-fi)
Transience (magic realism)
Black Heart (psych. thriller)
ENDURE (Dystopian)
THE END (Dystopian)
Horror Series:
Eat What You Kill (Book 1)
BAM (Book 2)
Eye For An Eye (Book 3)

Non-Fiction:
Wood Whisperer Volume 1
Wood Whisperer Volume 2
Wood Whisperer Volume 3
Giving Up (Short, autobiographical)

Visit Josef's web page for all purchase links and detailed book descriptions;
http://lakesidecaravanpark.wixsite.com/josef

ACKNOWLEDGMENTS

Once again, my editor deserves a shout out for her invaluable efforts in making my books come alive in the reader's eye.

CHAPTER ONE

"**Happy Birthday, pumpkin**. Sweet sixteen and never been kissed...I hope?"

"Mum, that's so lame," scolded Tara playfully.

"What? Who kissed you?" asked Clarice in a mild panic.

Tara unwrapped the present carefully, making sure not to tear the pretty wrapping paper. She would save it for decorating pages in her scrapbook. Inside the brightly printed paper, Tara found another layer even more exotic and colourful than the previous one.

"I suppose this is going to be paper all the way through, is it?"

"No, I just thought you would appreciate some more lovely paper for your scrapbook. I hunted all over to find a few designs I didn't think you had."

"They're gorgeous. I haven't seen this type at all. Where did you get them?"

"Sent away for them online."

Tara unwrapped the last layer to find the back of a picture frame. Her breath caught in her throat as she turned the frame over to see an oil painting depicting her and Arlon Grey, taken from Tara's favourite photo of them both. It was a perfect rendition of the pair, in a sensitive pose capturing his magnificent blue eyes and her happy grin in the arms of her beloved father. She stared at the painting for a long while as Clarice watched her.

Tara had never grieved for the man she adored beyond measure. The days, weeks and months following his disappearance were not as unhappy as her mother expected them to be for her daughter. She'd accepted the tragic event with stoicism and maturity beyond her years, but Clarice suspected that Tara was holding back.

The subject had been raised periodically and Tara seemed almost flippant in her responses, which troubled Clarice. Subsequent conversations with analysts and therapists and even hypnotherapy over the years failed to produce any of the expected emotions to emerge.

Clarice couldn't help herself, allowing the tears to come, while Tara remained dry-eyed.

"Oh, I hope I haven't done the wrong thing, princess. I thought you might like a painting to hang on your bedroom wall. I'll take it if you..."

"You'll do nothing of the bloody kind. It's mine. It's the best present in the world and I love it, Mum. Thank you," said Tara, leaning over to hug her mother.

Tara sat beside her mother on the austere lounge suite in the house they had inherited from Arlon Grey. She reverently touched the gilded frame and then placed her hand gently on his face in the painting.

"I miss him so much..." sobbed Clarice.

"I know, Mum."

Tara placed a comforting arm over Clarice's shoulder.

"Don't you?" asked Clarice in a sterner tone than she would have liked.

"Of course I do. What sort of a question is that?"

"You've never said anything, never cried, never spoken about him, nothing. Anyone would think you didn't give a fig," she blurted out, regretting her words the moment they left her mouth.

"I've never felt that he left. I always felt he was watching over us, me. Mum, I hear him sometimes," admitted Tara reluctantly.

"What? What do you mean?" cried Clarice in alarm.

"Oh, don't go having a cow. I don't mean I hear voices. No, I mean I hear him sometimes, in my sleep, in my mind like I could on the island. Of course I miss that he isn't here in the flesh, but I just never felt his loss like you did. I've never felt he was truly gone."

"Really?"

"Absolutely. I was sad when it happened, but...I don't know, it's just that..."

"What?" Clarice insisted.

"You know when you're alone in the living room, for instance, but don't feel *lonely* because you know there's someone else in another room of the house: in another bedroom or bathroom. It's like that. Somehow, I can't see him or touch him, but I know he's there. Whenever I've had a problem all I had to do was think of him and I would get an answer, or the problem would be solved somehow. When I was bullied that time?" Clarice nodded. "I spoke to Dad in my dreams that night and the next day I seemed to know what to say to make the problem go away."

"You never told me that."

"I couldn't figure out what happened exactly, so I didn't want to start telling you something that made no sense. You think he's happy, Mum?"

"Oh, what a question. Is that an existentialist question or something?"

"You know I'm not religious, Mum. We both know where he went."

"You believe he went into that..."

"Other dimension, Mum. Say it."

"Other dimension? Is that truly what you think happened?"

"Of course, don't you?"

"I never knew what to make of it."

"That's because you didn't want to handle it. If you think about it logically, it's the only explanation. His use of the energy caused the increase in its presence, or intensity, and drew him into the other dimension. Maybe he survived. Maybe he learned to use it more. Maybe he found a way to get closer to this dimension where he can speak to me sometimes if the planets are aligned or some such thing. You know, a cosmic connection?"

"And maybe that's just a whole heap of wishful thinking, young lady."

"It's why I don't feel sad like you, Mum."

Clarice's mobile phone buzzed and vibrated on the marble

benchtop in the kitchen.

"That's the business mobile, I'd better get it. Could mean work for me."

"Don't know why you won't take some of my inheritance money so you don't have to rely on that income anymore. I'd still have heaps left over."

Clarice rose from the sofa, ignoring Tara's generosity, to fetch the phone that was still vibrating so much it was likely to drop off the benchtop.

"BAM Detective Agency, how may I help you?" she said into the phone. "Yes, this is Clarice Grey. Yes, that's how it's spelt, why...? I'm sorry? Look... No, you may not know my daughter's name. I am ending this call... It... What happened? When was this? Every night? My name and hers? Can you send me some photos? Give me your number just in case it disappears from my phone. I'm technically challenged that way. I'll give you a call once I've studied the photos and discussed it with someone."

Clarice remained pensive as she disconnected the call. She stood in the kitchen shaking her head slowly from side to side.

"What was it, Mum?"

"Hmm? Oh, just a business call."

"Oh, golly gee, that's so informative...NOT!"

"Tara Grey, you don't need to be told everything, you know?"

"No, I don't know. Whatever happened to 'sharing everything and not holding back'?"

"Well, you haven't, have you?"

"What?"

"You never said anything about what you just told me. About feeling Arlon with you, and thinking he went to that other place."

"I always thought you were intelligent enough to assume he went there and that I didn't need to explain."

"Nothing simple about it. No telling where he went."

"Oh, I get it now!" said Tara angrily.

"What? What is it you think you get, missy?" challenged

Clarice.

"You're angry with him because you think he could have done something to prevent it."

"Nonsense..."

"Yes, you are. You think he allowed himself to go or even encouraged it."

"Well, he certainly had the power, didn't he?" Clarice admitted.

"When you open Pandora's box, you don't necessarily have the skills to operate everything you find in there. Daddy would never have intentionally left us. He loved us with all his heart."

"Don't be so naïve, Tara. He couldn't love. Maybe he can finally express love wherever he ended up. Maybe he is a happy man at last. He wasn't one for this world, that's for sure."

The ping on her phone alerted Clarice to the incoming message. Swiping the screen, she furrowed her brow as she concentrated on the small images.

"Mum? Is everything all right?"

"Damn! I don't want to ask, but you're so much better at this tech stuff than I am. How do I get these pictures from my mobile to my computer so I can enlarge them?"

"Mum, how can you run a professional agency and not know how to do that?"

"Don't help your mother, then, if that's how you're going to be."

"Give it here," demanded Tara with a sigh and a smile.

Clarice watched her daughter unfold herself from the sofa to stand in front of her. Clarice had to look up to view her daughter's features. At sixteen, Tara towered over her mother, with long legs and blossoming curves, accentuated by tight jeans and a white T-shirt. Her long hair shone with an anthracite brilliance, highlighting and framing the perfectly-proportioned face and enigmatic green eyes.

Tara accepted the proffered mobile and quickly attached it to Clarice's laptop using a cable from the kitchen drawer. She set them both up on the kitchen bench and began the process of transferring the pictures from the phone.

Tara's sharp intake of breath told Clarice that she had succeeded in the task and opened the file to view the pictures. She didn't immediately say anything, wanting Tara's take on the photos without influencing her in any way.

"Mum? Why is my full name, Tara Blaze-Grey, emblazoned on this bloke's walls alongside yours?"

"He claims they reappear every morning no matter how many times he removes them or repaints the wall."

"How long has it been happening and where is this?"

"Six years."

"Jesus, that's..."

"Yes. That's exactly the length of time that Arlon's been missing," whispered Clarice sadly.

"Where?" asked Tara with growing concern.

"A little seaside town called Tannum Sands."

"Mum, that's where..."

"I know," said Clarice quickly.

"Is it the same house?"

"I don't know that yet."

"Do his parents still live there?"

"No, they moved to Brisbane with Arlon when he was still fairly young. I think they're in a retirement home now. I've only ever spoken to them once since we were married. That was bloody awkward, I tell you. Horrible people. I'm glad we never had to do our duty by visiting them regularly. Not that we were together all that long," said Clarice with a sigh.

"So, if it is, how have our names mysteriously appeared on the walls of Daddy's childhood home for the six years that he's been missing?" asked Tara quietly.

"We're being offered the brief to find out, according to the message on the phone. That fellow said he finally made the connection with the names when he came across our magazine ad with my name as the contact on it in a doctor's waiting room."

"I knew it," Tara said almost to herself.

"Tara Grey, I will not have you going down that road. I forbid you to think like that."

"Like what?" asked Tara pointedly.

"You know what I'm talking about," replied Clarice, with her fists on her hips.

Tara laughed.

"What's so funny?"

"Daddy always said not to go up against you when you strike that pose," said Tara, with a further giggle. She adopted a more serious tone. "He was the only one who used to call me by my full name. It has to be him."

"Princess, I don't want you to get your hopes up," said Clarice, embracing Tara. "It will just end in heartache for us both. I'll tell him we don't want the case."

"I'll go there myself if you do that," warned Tara, in a voice so low that Clarice almost missed it.

CHAPTER TWO

"Ahem!"

Tara turned from the window out of which she had just climbed, with a yelp of surprise, given the hour.

"Mum? Jeez, you nearly gave me a heart attack sneaking up on me like that."

"Don't you go trying to turn the tables on me, young lady. You're the one sneaking out of your bedroom window at midnight. I'm just the one catching you at it. Care to explain yourself?"

Tara squinted in the glare of the torchlight. She sighed dramatically as she lowered her father's backpack on to the ground at her feet.

"I have to go, Mum. I know it's Dad trying to reach us."

"So you think you should go by yourself in the middle of the night, without so much as a word to me?"

"I was going to call," Tara admitted with a shrug.

"And just how were you going to get there? Steal the car? The car you aren't licensed to drive yet?"

"No. I was going to hitch."

"Are you insane? Hitch? A young girl hitching a ride in the middle of the night! Your father would...well, he wouldn't be impressed at all."

"Dad would've told me to follow my hunch... Wait a minute, why are you dressed?"

"Arlon Grey would *not* have agreed to his sixteen-year-old daughter attempting to hitchhike anywhere at any time, Tara, and neither do I. So get yourself in the car this minute. We have a long way to travel."

"Wait, what?"

"You think I'm too old to know what a young, impetuous girl

of your age might do? I accepted the brief after you'd gone to bed. Graham Bellows is expecting us."

"I don't believe this. You knew?"

"Of course I knew. The car's packed with our gear, including yours. Take the pack you have there if you want. I've made up sandwiches and coffee to save us money on the road. I don't want us eating in those horrible roadside diners."

"You mean it? You accepted the brief?"

"Don't look so excited, young lady. You have to agree to a few ground rules before we go, otherwise, I call and cancel and you will be under strict observation for the foreseeable future."

"What rules?"

"First and foremost is that I am the lead investigator, and you are accompanying me only as an assistant, with no say whatsoever in the running of the investigation or any authority when it comes to dealing with the client. You will do *as* I say, *when* I say, with none of your usual back-talk. You will not do anything without my prior approval, and will under no circumstances attempt anything on your own."

"Is that it?"

"I'm sure I'll think of a few more things as we go," said Clarice, with her hands planted firmly on her hips.

"What about bug-a-lugs?" Tara asked suddenly, with more than a hint of guilt for not having thought about him earlier.

"Already at the Coopers'. They're happy to take care of him until we return. Mary Cooper has been itching to look after him ever since they moved next door."

"Bet old Bob won't be too happy about that."

"If it makes his wife happy and reduces her grief from the loss of their child, he'll be more than welcome in their home. Well?"

"Well, what?"

"Do you agree to my conditions?"

"Can't I help, even a little bit?"

"I said you'll be my assistant, didn't I? Just don't try anything without my say-so."

"Okay, I agree. Are you really all packed and ready to go?"

"Only needs us in the car to get going on our way to Tannum Sands. Only..."

"What?"

"Please don't get your hopes up, sweetie."

"I don't have to; I know it's him, Mum. He's probably figured out a way..."

"Tara Blaze-Grey! I will not have you repeating those absurd notions to the Bellows, especially the wife and daughter. Is that clear?"

"Another rule you just made up?"

"Yes, and there'll be more. I just haven't thought of them yet."

"How can I agree or comply with rules that aren't even in existence yet?"

"Learn to live with it. Like it or not, I have a business to run and that sort of talk can get us thrown out of a job."

"Not likely. You're the co-founder of the Bizarre and Mysterious Detective Agency. I've seen the types you deal with, Mum. Most of them are whackos."

"Whackos that pay our mortgage and put food on the table. Finished?"

"Can't think of another thing to add to that or say in my defence."

"You'll keep," said Clarice with a warm smile. "Get going. I have the caravan hitched up and ready to roll."

"Oh no! Not the pop-top? Can't swing a dead cat in that thing."

"Just as well we aren't taking any cats, then, dead or alive. We can't stay in the client's house and motels are expensive, especially with a Nipper carnival in progress at the weekend."

"We aren't staying in a caravan park, are we? I hate those community shower blocks."

"Mr Bellows has space in his back yard for our van. We can use a bathroom he has in a shed outside. Or you can go for a swim in the ocean."

"Oh, goody," she said with a sarcastic smirk.

"Stay here then, Tara. If your daddy means that little to you I can't understand what all the fuss is about."

Tara sucked the air between her teeth. "Mum! That was a horrible thing to say."

"You were perfectly willing to risk your life by hitchhiking, but can't put up with staying in a caravan for a short time while we investigate this matter? Make up your mind, Tara. This isn't a picnic or a holiday. I'm accepting you as my assistant under sufferance, only because I know how you feel and the lengths you'll go to if there is even the slightest chance there may be news of your father."

"Don't you want to know?"

"You know better than to ask me that. Now, in the car or off to the Coopers' to join your brother?"

"No way I'm staying here with...them."

"Get in the car then and kindly watch your manners, young lady. I don't intend to fight with you all the way. Lose the attitude and remember to follow my rules."

Clarice turned to enter their inherited, early-model Toyota Prado. Tara threw her pack into the rear seat and entered the passenger side. The moment she sat down, she donned a set of earplugs to listen to tunes on her phone.

CHAPTER THREE

Tannum Sands was a small coastal village servicing the huge number of itinerant workers lured by the promise of employment in either the alumina plant or the power station during Arlon Grey's youth. It grew exponentially as both of those industries expanded, requiring more and more workers. Boyne Island and Tannum Sands were joined by the construction of a bridge over the Boyne river, which had previously separated the two townships for many years.

The town would have been unrecognisable to the Greys had they returned. Harbouring only a few hundred back then, it had grown to a population of over 10,000 permanent residents, divided equally between the twin towns. Graham Bellows' beach bungalow was nestled between towering palm trees near the mouth of the Boyne river, affording him spectacular views of the river mouth and the open ocean. No doubt it would be highly-prized real estate in the not too distant future, if it wasn't already.

The bungalow was constructed from a timber frame, lined on the exterior with fibre-cement sheeting. Interior linings consisted of VJ lining boards with a whitewashed finish. The flooring was a garish yellow/orange shag pile in the living areas and utilitarian linoleum in the kitchen. All the furnishings screamed of mid-seventies, with harsh lime green cushions on the cane sofa, orange vinyl chairs surrounding the laminated kitchen table and matching kitchen cupboards.

Clarice knocked tentatively on the bright orange front door. Tara stood by her side nervously, switching her weight from one foot to the other. Taking note of the unkempt gardens and faded paint on the walls, Clarice concluded that the Bellows' family had more pressing concerns than gardening and house maintenance.

It came as no shock to her then when Graham Bellows, aged only thirty-three, opened the front door looking more like a man in his sixties. His harried features spoke of the strain he and his family had endured for the previous six years of their occupancy.

"Clarice Grey from the BAM Detective Agency," she announced quickly before he slammed the door back in her face thinking her a hawker of some kind. "This is my assistant and daughter, Tara."

"Oh, right. I almost forgot you were coming. Sorry, bad night...again. Come in."

"Thank you. If you don't mind my saying so, you look terrible, Mr Bellows."

"No, I don't mind," he said, leading them down the narrow hall to the rear kitchen. "We don't get much sleep around here anymore and it's taking its toll. Can I get you some coffee...or a cold drink?"

"Coffee for me and some cold water for Tara would be terrific, thank you. Will your wife and daughter be joining us?"

"Julie's with Cynthia in Gladstone for the day. She'll be back later this afternoon, possibly. Sugar and milk?"

"Two and white for me, yes," replied Clarice as she took the proffered seat.

"Wow, these colours are so retro," said Tara brightly, taking in the kitchen decor.

Graham turned with a strained smile. "It's the reason we purchased the house. We just loved all the old funky colours."

They all settled into an uncomfortable silence while Graham made the coffee. Once he had given Tara a tall glass of chilled water, he sat down with his coffee.

"Coffee okay?"

"Very nice, thank you." Clarice waited a moment or two for him to begin. "Why don't you tell us what's been happening, Mr Bellows?"

"Graham, please."

"Okay, Graham. Go ahead and explain the reason you called us."

"Ghosts," he said simply with a shrug, shaking his head at the absurd notion.

"Care to elaborate?"

"We bought this old house nearly ten years ago and the first year was just...heaven. It was fantastic. The weather, the beach, the views. We were so happy that we decided to have a child. Cynthia was born a year later. When Cynthia was around two the troubles began. We thought it was her, of course. She'd wake up at night screaming as though she was being attacked by something. She spoke of them, the monsters, and we both thought it was a thing children went through at that age until we saw the names appearing on the walls.

"It got worse and worse until we had to sedate her to get her to sleep. We've seen any number of specialists and psychiatrists, but no one has been able to diagnose a specific problem."

"Neither you nor your wife have seen whatever it is that's disturbing her?" asked Clarice.

"We've seen enough other stuff to know it wasn't just Cynthia. The names, your names, started appearing on the walls every night. No matter what I do, paint them over, wash them off, nothing stops them from coming back. Noises, horrible sounds you wouldn't believe, the house shaking and groaning. We're at our wits' end. My daughter has to sleep at my sister's house in Gladstone now. She's too terrified to come back. Julie visits her almost every other day. I...we...don't know what else to do."

"Have you tried..."

"Everything from clairvoyants to exorcists. No one can stop this crap from happening. We can't afford to move after all the money we spent trying to get Cynthia better. You are our very last hope. I've sold my car and my boat to meet your expenses. They were the last of my possessions of any value. I don't even know how long my job will last as I'm such a wreck. I can't function normally anymore. Most nights I sleep on the beach just to get some rest."

Clarice took a moment to examine their host. He appeared haggard and entirely sincere. He sported a scraggly beard on his gaunt face. She assumed he would be quite a good-looking man with a solid build if he had not lost so much weight, which made him seem sickly. That he was at the end of his tolerance level was evident. Clarice was suddenly concerned for her daughter's welfare.

"Can you help us?" asked Graham, with a note of desperation in his voice.

"I'm not sure. I have to wait and see what happens for myself, then proceed from there. Has anything happened to physically harm anyone at this point?"

"You think I look like this normally?"

"I can tell that the mental strain is affecting you. What I want to know is if anyone has been physically attacked?" she asked delicately.

"My daughter suffered scratches and bruises that we can't explain. Other than that, no," Graham admitted sadly, thinking he was being judged a crackpot. "Sorry to waste your..."

"You misunderstood my intentions, Graham. I am not trying to belittle anything you've said. I am not here to make a judgement call on your character or your family situation, or anything the authorities might concern themselves with. You saw the name of our detective agency? That's what we deal with, and the people who suffer from those types of problems. Believe me, I've faced some weird stuff in the time we've been operating. You strike me as a no-nonsense kind of guy and all this is very much out of your comfort zone, even to talk about or acknowledge?"

"Got that right. I don't believe in ghosts...or didn't. I don't know what it is, but it isn't normal, and I just want it to end before we go broke and lose this house. Before I lose my family, my mind, or both."

"Tell us about the names," suggested Clarice respectfully.

"Every night, like clockwork, those names start appearing on the walls down the hallway. Every day I wash them off or paint over them and they come right back."

"Paint?" she asked.

"I wish. No, blood."

"Blood? Are you sure?"

"Ick!" exclaimed Tara.

"Tara, that's enough," Clarice rebuked mildly.

"Yeah, it's blood all right. Sent a sample away to get it tested. My friend phoned me himself to tell me the results. Blood," said Graham with sadness.

"Human?"

"Yep."

"Did they perform a DNA analysis?"

"Yeah, they did that too."

"So, our names and nothing else?"

"Yeah, just your names. I nearly jumped out of my skin when I saw your name in the magazine at the doctor's office. I was marking time, waiting for my daughter to come out of a session with one of the shrinks she was seeing. I wasn't even reading it, if truth be told. I was just trying to keep my mind busy and my hands doing something normal. I glanced over the advertisement and thought it was some oddball outfit looking to rip off unsuspecting victims...sorry," he said with an apologetic shrug, "and then your name hit me right between the eyes. There it was in black and white: Clarice Grey. I gave up trying to phone all the C. Greys in the phone listings a few years before that. Do you have any idea how many there are in Australia?"

"No, I don't," she admitted.

"A lot! I gathered the courage to ring you the next evening. I hope you can do something for me, because if I find out you're some crackpot con-artists I..."

"Graham, what we do is investigate the bizarre and the mysterious. We do not have a perfect track record for solving every case. Some are just inexplicable. We've uncovered a few fraudsters during our investigations. We even had one client try to use our involvement as some sort of endorsement for her nefarious activities, which included spiritual connections with the deceased and fortune-telling, at a significant cost, I might add. While I am somewhat drawn to the paranormal, Graham, I am probably as sceptical as most when I take on a case. I offer a form of guarantee which you will not read about in my advertisements. If you feel that my company is in any way negligent or falsely representing its mission statement, you will be entitled to a full refund."

"Have you ever dealt with anything like this?"

"Yes and no. I've investigated spiritual sightings before now. I confess I've debunked more claims than I've proven. In fact, I've never proven the existence of spirits or ghosts in any of my past dealings. My sole purpose in establishing the agency, and maintaining it after the disappearance of my husband, was to provide a point of contact for persons with problems that fell outside the realm of the acceptable: the 'normal'."

"That explains me and my problem to a T. Police won't have a bar of it, despite the results of the tests coming back as human blood, despite them seeing the writing on the wall every time I called them. I even had a copper staying with us one night who didn't hear or see anything, but the writing turned up there just the same. He had no explanation other than it was probably a human doing it for a gag: 'probably me', he said. They won't even come here anymore. I can't speak to anyone but underlings if I call the station. They started following me around, handing me traffic tickets if I did the slightest thing wrong, like coming to a rolling stop at a stop sign."

"Well, I'd like to set our camper up in your yard, if I may, and get ready for an all-nighter in your hallway?"

CHAPTER FOUR

"You didn't tell him," said Tara after their camper was set up and they were relaxing inside with a bite to eat.

"Tell him what?"

"About the connection, about this being..."

"He doesn't need to know. He's haunted enough, in case you didn't see what I saw earlier."

"What do you think about all this?"

"Too early to make any assumptions or guesses. Any chance you might eat your food instead of playing with it?"

"I'm too wound up to think about eating, Mum."

"You shouldn't get your hopes up, Tara. He's been gone for six years and isn't likely to be showing up ever again, let alone in his childhood home."

"It's just too much of a coincidence for it not to be connected. It has to be him, Mum, it just has to be," said Tara sadly.

"You miss him terribly, don't you?"

"Don't you?"

"Every hour of every day, dear. What I can't do is hold out hope or give up on the life we have. We had some good times, didn't we? I gave you love, didn't I?"

"How can you even ask that?"

"It seems that way sometimes. I feel I'm coming off as second best."

"Mum! That's just not true," Tara exclaimed.

"Isn't it? You've been overly quiet from the time he disappeared. You've never once opened up to me about it, and even when we share a cuddle I see that distant look in your eyes, that unfulfilled wish that it was Arlon you were hugging instead of me. This is the first time I've seen you so animated, so alive, and sparkling with that vivacity you showed when we first met you."

Tara took a moment to absorb what her mother was saying, shaking her head in denial first, then gradually changing it to a nod as she realised the truth of the statement. She ate a little of her hot dog without any enthusiasm. Clarice waited patiently for her daughter to arrive at a conclusion. She knew her well enough to know that Tara was tossing up all the information to test it for holes, untruths.

"Sorry, Mum. I haven't been a very good daughter, have I?"

"Nonsense. I never once complained. I was only ever concerned for you, Tara. I'll admit to being a little bit jealous of what you had with him. Then I think about the joy you two shared during that glorious year together and I have to chide myself for having such ungracious thoughts. Arlon Grey was a difficult man to love, yet somehow you did love him and he reciprocated, which was very surprising, given his condition. I did envy you two that."

"I do love you, Mum, more than I ever did my natural mother. I'm sorry you feel I didn't love you as much as Daddy. I don't think it's true," she offered half-heartedly.

"You still call him Daddy?" asked Clarice with a smile. "See? There's the difference. I'm relegated to Mum these days, whereas you still call him by the name you used back then. I lose, even when he hasn't been around for all the time we've had together."

"It isn't a competition, Mum. I get what you're saying, though. But living with you, as your daughter, has given me some of the happiest moments of my life. I've always loved you. You've been a great mother and friend."

"Shall we?"

Tara nodded. The pair exited the van to join Graham in the house. He sat at the kitchen table with a full glass of liquor: not his first, by the look of it. Clarice frowned at the half-full bottle of Jack on the kitchen counter. His fear was palpable, escaping his pores as a tangible, unpleasant odour. Tara wrinkled her nose when she also detected the strange scent. The pair sat without voicing the opinions dancing on the tips of their tongues.

Wordlessly, Graham held his glass aloft in Clarice's direction, inviting her to partake. Wisely, she declined without comment or a sign of disapproval. She understood his need to drown his fear, to attempt a show of Dutch courage in the face of strangers. His nerves had been worn to a frazzle over the years and his face showed the lines of worry etched into his once handsome features.

Earlier, Clarice had set up a phalanx of microphones, cameras and other equipment throughout the house, all geared to begin recording when activated by movement, sound or heat signature. The only place not wired was the kitchen, where they would all remain for the night. Graham had convinced her that nothing ever occurred in the kitchen, with the proviso that the condition could change. Nothing seemed to be set in stone. He explained that nothing about any of it was in the least bit routine or predictable.

Clarice warned them to keep their conversation to an absolute minimum and to be extremely quiet should they need to convey something of importance. The equipment she utilised was highly sensitive with a respectable range. Although she believed they were not likely to activate the sensors from the kitchen, she preferred to err on the side of caution and did not want to thwart a nightly occurrence with unnecessary and frivolous chatter.

Tara sipped from a fruit juice popper, while Clarice drank coffee from her stainless steel flask. The night was dark, without moon or starlight penetrating the thick layer of clouds that rolled across the sky late in the afternoon, portending a storm. Clarice smiled as she thought about the appropriateness of a storm to accompany the visitation: if it came. The crack of thunder took them by surprise...except for Graham. He shook his head when Clarice peered skyward. Tara's eyes were wide as saucers.

Graham gave the females a weary, knowing nod to indicate that the evening's festivities had begun. He wondered why they were so surprised. He'd warned them several times about the noises accompanying the visitations. He could see that the attractive woman thought she'd heard thunder, but Graham knew better. It was only the beginning of another torturous night.

When the louvred windows began trembling in their frames, Tara thought she might wet herself. The clap of thunder that preceded the shaking had ended moments ago. The overhead lights began flickering in time to the trembling. A bass sound began to thrum through the walls and floorboards: a deep, resonant 'glunking' sound that seemed to penetrate her body with its reverberations. Tara rose quickly, indicating to her mother a desperate need to pee. Clarice nodded uncertainly, attempting to remain as calm and detached as possible.

She observed Graham taking everything in without a hint of surprise showing on his glum features. He raised his glass in a silent toast, welcoming her to his nightmare. He drained the last of his glass's contents before rising to top it up with a shot straight from the bottle. Clarice gestured her acceptance of the earlier offer. He poured her a generous two fingers of the liquor. When he spied her two fingers separating to form a wide V, he conceded by giving her the extra shot with a knowing smirk and a nod.

He was relieved that she was experiencing some of what he'd had to endure for what seemed a lifetime. Not that he'd believed he'd imagined any of it. He was long past thinking in those sceptical terms. While he was unable to explain or rationalise it, he had come to accept it as being very, very real.

Graham was also pleased that his wife and daughter were nowhere near the place. There had been a steady progression in intensity of the events over the last few months. An escalation of noise levels and accompanying incidents had him fearing worse to come. Before he had spied the advertisement in that magazine, he had made up his mind to burn the house down, regardless of the investigation by the insurance company that would surely follow.

He surrendered to the fact that he would be discovered as the arsonist. The local police were champing at the bit to see him locked up for the trouble he'd caused them, calling them out in the press as incompetent cowards. He had long ago resigned himself to a prison term. As long as his wife and daughter were safe, he would accept anything. The house was no longer insured,anyway. He didn't have the funds to keep up with the rising premiums, despite never having made a claim. He understood that the insurance broker he used had a relationship with one of the local coppers.

Admiring her strength of character, Graham toasted Clarice. If what she was experiencing in his house was in any way like events she dealt with regularly, he had her deepest respect. Nothing could be more bizarre and mysterious, in his opinion, than the nightly events he'd suffered year after year. He winced as the bile rose from his gut. The reflux began as his drinking increased. It caused him no end of discomfort, despite the medication his doctor prescribed.

He sat again with a heavy thud onto the chair, smiling a question at the woman opposite. She nodded in acknowledgement of his harrowing experiences and drank deeply of the strong liquid. Flashing lights, and the sound of her recording equipment gearing into life in the hallway, drew Clarice's attention away from the defeated man. She would dearly have loved to remove herself from his depressing presence to investigate the disturbance, but resisted the urge, knowing she would only interfere.

Tara returned with a questioning frown, but stopped short of speaking it when she saw her mother's finger pressed to her lips.

The lights snapped out. The power died. All sounds bar one ceased.

Glunk, glunk, glunk.

CHAPTER FIVE

"Leave?"

"Believe me, that's new," Graham whispered.

It was morning and a steady drizzle pattered on the tin roof. The electricity had returned several hours after the thunder clap that wasn't. Nothing they had attempted prior to that could induce the power to return.

When it was light enough, they viewed the wall in the hallway where the writing always appeared. It had been significantly altered. Smeared over the top of Clarice and Tara's names was the word *LEAVE* in a different hand to the letters underneath.

" Is this warping normal?" asked Clarice.

"You mean the wall? No, that's new, as well," answered Graham. "Although other walls at different times have shown slight buckling. Nothing like this. I won't have to burn this place down if this keeps up."

"Why would you think of burning it down?"

"A cleansing by fire seems only natural for what's going on here. If that ghost is telling me to leave then I should be bloody-well heeding its advice."

"Is it?"

"Is it what?"

"Is it meant for you?"

"My house."

"Our names," explained Clarice pointedly.

"Mum..."

"Hush, Tara."

"But..."

"Remember the rules?"

"Really?"

"Why don't you go for a swim? You love the ocean,"

suggested Clarice in a warm tone.

"Since when?"

"Tara!" Clarice warned.

"It's raining."

"And? Afraid you'll get wet going for a swim? Besides, the sun will be out before you know it. You need a wash, young lady. Or would you rather...?"

"I'm not going in there for all the tea in China," Tara uttered with a shudder.

"Well, then, off you go and don't hurry back. Take a tenner from my purse to go visit the shops after."

"Wow, that's generous of you."

"Sarcasm does not become you, Tara Blaze-Grey."

Tara took the not-so-subtle hint as a sign that her mother would soon be shipping her back home if she didn't play ball. Tara zipped her mouth tightly and walked outside to the van. She would find a quiet moment later that evening to talk to her mother about a theory she had: not a theory exactly, more an observation. If she was right, it encouraged her to be optimistic.

Although the events the previous evening scared the crap out of her, she remained cheerful in the morning after she was finally allowed to see the writing. The other thing? Well, she wasn't about to venture an opinion on the bathroom. No way would she ever step foot inside that bathroom again after what they found there.

Clarice walked down the hall toward the main bedroom, stopping short at the door to the bathroom on her left. She steeled herself for the sight of the interior for the second time that morning. The stench was indescribable as she inched open the door on its remaining hinge.

It was a slaughterhouse. Blood spattered the white walls, white shower tiles, the white enamel bath, ceiling, window, light, everything. The porcelain toilet and cistern were smashed, with dangerously sharp shards littering the tiled floor and blood puddling in the new depressions. Worst by far, in Clarice's opinion, was the lump of conically-shaped flesh resting in one corner.

The police would have to be called in, despite their reluctance to attend the Bellows' residence. The evidence was irrefutable and entirely unconnected with Graham Bellows. Clarice would testify to the fact that he had been out cold in the kitchen. Although she had been unable to see him in the pitch-black night, she'd heard him readily enough.

Tara had been told to go to the van to get some sleep. Clarice had remained in the kitchen with Graham until dawn cast its pallid light through the dirty louvres. He had fallen asleep a few hours earlier and snored up a storm in his drunken stupor. The bottle of Jack was empty. Clarice had not attempted to wake him. She was rattled by the events of the evening, no question about it, and had no wish for Graham Bellows to witness her discomfort. It would not compare to how she felt when she viewed the results of the visitation.

When the police finally arrived, they performed their tasks cursorily, taking few notes and fewer samples as evidence. The forensic lab was not notified. The blood and flesh were accepted as animalian by the attending officers without so much as a second thought. Their animosity towards Clarice's client was painfully obvious. The disdain dripping from them with every word spoken made Clarice seethe.

"Have I not made it very clear that my client had nothing whatever to do with the events we described?" asked Clarice.

The senior constable (not a detective, Clarice noted) arched his shoulders back in a confrontational stance, towering over the diminutive form of the annoying woman in front of him as he approached.

"Well now, little lady, why don't you...?"

"Don't you dare 'little lady' me. I'll have you up on charges before you can blink...officer!" Clarice declared, with her hands planted firmly on her hips, ringlets of gold bouncing around her cherubic features. "That sort of misogynistic horseshit hasn't been tolerated for some time now, or have you forgotten, Constable Hart? Or hasn't that bit of legislature filtered down to this little backwater and you outdated law enforcement 'professionals' yet?"

"Now you just hold on there..."

"I will not hold on. Just so you know, I am recording this conversation, and I will not hold back when you're sitting in the jury box or at a disciplinary hearing."

Senior Constable Peter Hart pushed back a few strands of his greying hair over his thinning pate. He was nearing retirement age and begrudging every last moment he would have to spend in service to the ugly public before he was finally free. His lucrative retirement pension depended on him staying to the very last day. He wanted to scream at the bitch, hit her, make her pay for the threat, a threat that could see him lose his pension if he were found guilty of the charges she implied.

He rued the day that females were allowed on the force. He rued the day they were permitted to participate in patrols, to be allowed to partner up with veterans, to take down perps...everything. The whole affirmative action thing, the #MeToo movement, angered him deeply. After his messy divorce, that wiped him out financially, he no longer had time for females.

Peter Hart was old school. He had joined the force back in the day when men were men, and police officers did not brook the sort of garbage that the public got away with presently. He remembered delivering 'messages' to perpetrators of minor crimes back in the day: messages that were heard very clearly and often prevented further transgressions by said perpetrators.

He hated what the force had become, what the men of the force were obligated to conform to. Discrimination, misogyny, prejudice, racial inequality, profiling...the list was endless. It wasn't an officer's fault if a bloody native couldn't handle being locked up for wrongdoing. If they opted to take their lives while in custody, how could that be in any way construed as being the fault of the police or correction officers?

Good bloody riddance, as far as he was concerned. One less trouble-maker off the streets. He cared even less for the snotty little bitch confronting him at the moment. While he would have given anything to give her a bloody lip for the shit she was sprouting, he held his anger in check, knowing his future depended on it. The only thing his ex-wife did not get from the divorce was any claim to his super. His lawyer and a personal friend had managed to get his super off the table in light of everything else she'd stripped from him.

It was touch and go for a while as to whether he would survive the divorce. He lived in hovels, barely able to cover the pitiful rent, utilities and food. He lived off baked beans and rice for years. To add insult to injury she managed to slap him with a restraining order when he tried to talk reason with her one drunken night. That one incident had almost destroyed his career and his pension. If not for the good relations he enjoyed with the chief, a mate from the academy, he would have found himself out of the force.

The memory of that incident still simmered in him after years. Fortunately, it also had the effect of forcing him to calm his demeanour, to squash his anger and resentment of...everything, back down into his gut, where it fermented into a roiling but controlled tempest that caused more than a few ulcers and elevated his blood pressure.

Senior Constable Peter Hart and his junior partner of five long-suffering months, Constable Sarah Vaughn, had been called out to the Bellows' home on more occasions than they cared to remember. His bellicose demeanour had not aided in their relationship with the complainant. His predilections had not gained him any sympathy from his partner, either, which meant he had no choice but to stand down if he wanted to reach the brass ring: his pension.

"All right, best we tone down the negative tension here so that we're all on the same page," suggested Peter, biting back the insult he would have loved to hurl at the diminutive woman right after delivering a punishing left hook.

That left hook had brought all the woes of the world down on his shoulders when he gave it to his ex-wife during that moment of drunken insanity. That one moment of ignominious shame gave her a tool of blackmail to strip him of all his worldly goods: *his* worldly goods, because she'd never worked a day in her life. She threatened to take his house, car, dogs, boat, savings...the lot. If he agreed to it, she would not press charges. He would escape the court case that would see him lose everything else.

It galled him no end to swallow down his rage, to appear impotent in front of a female who had him by the balls...again. He bit down hard on the building anger to manufacture a look of humility and cooperation. His smile looked more like a grimace of pain to Clarice.

"Well, if you want us all on the same page, I suggest you start reading the book, because the law book has evidently escaped your perusal of late. Bullying my client with false traffic infringements every time he's out driving, and turning a blind eye to what's happening here, goes against your charter somewhat, don't you think?"

"You know how many times we've been called to a domestic disturbance in this house...ma'am?"

"You don't think the evidence here qualifies as something more than a domestic disturbance? There's enough blood in there for several bodies to have bled out. I looked up some of your last reports and nowhere does it mention that the blood found on the walls every night was human. I don't think you've even troubled yourself to order a DNA test, have you?"

"Could have been his blood," he muttered.

"Did you search his person for signs of self-inflicted wounds? A simple DNA test would have decided the matter had you bothered to perform your duty."

"Ma'am, you need to dial down the hostility. We are here doing our job for about the twentieth time we've been called to this address. Apart from words on a wall...your names, it turns out, there hasn't been anything to investigate. No sign of foul play, no body, mutilated or otherwise. Loud noises in the night, shaking beds, vague outlines and shimmering visions are not in our purview. We aren't the paranormal police. Not the Ghostbusters of Hollywood fame," said Constable Sarah Vaughn.

"Not sure why you're standing up for this male chauvinist, but does that blood in there and that lump of flesh look anything but real to you? Nothing imaginary or paranormal about clear, hard evidence, which neither of you bagged and tagged, by the way. Pretty standard police procedure in Brisbane. Do they do things differently here? No need for facts and evidence to get in the way of your conclusions based on guesswork? My client..."

"Sorry, tell me again, who are you? His lawyer? Oh, no, that's right. You're just some private dick from out of town interfering with official police matters. Care for a little counter charge of obstruction?" warned the junior officer.

"Asking you to take evidence is obstructing your duties? That's a good one. That one is going to get laughed out of court so quickly your head will spin. If..."

"Enough!" bawled Graham. "If you aren't going to do anything constructive about this, you need to go. I have one hell of a hangover. If you don't stop all this crap I'm going to throw up, and I don't have a bathroom I can do that in. Meaning, I'll have to run outside and throw up in your patrol vehicle," threatened Graham from the same seat at the kitchen table where he had spent the evening.

Clarice smiled when she saw the look of horror registering on the faces of the beleaguered cops. The thought of sitting in puke or smelling it all day had them backpedalling quickly.

"There isn't much we can do here aside from investigating an act of vandalism. Without a body... Wait a minute. Where is your wife?"

"The same place she was the last time you asked me that question," replied Graham in a bored tone.

"Is she going to be there when I ring to confirm that fact?"

"I don't see why not. Why? Oh! You think the only possible explanation for all this would be that I killed my wife and possibly my daughter. Pathetic. Get out! NOW!"

"We'll get going, all right. Remember it was you who kicked us out next time you think about calling us, Bellows," said Hart with a sneer.

"So if a body does show up we shouldn't call the police?" asked Clarice.

"Only if you want us to arrest him for murder. Otherwise, you can keep your fantasies to yourself. I want nothing more to do with this nonsense, you or him," Peter spat as he turned and gestured to his junior partner to leave.

"Good bloody riddance," Graham said once the door had closed.

"You shouldn't antagonise them. Comes a time they might be handy to have on our side," explained Clarice.

"Six years of crap I've put up with from them, those protectors of the public. Arrogant pricks! You have no idea what they've put my family through. Getting so we can't show our faces around here, they've bad-mouthed us so efficiently, ostracising us from our neighbours as though we're nothing but crackpots. I need a drink..."

"Not if you want me to stay here and help, you don't. You aren't any use to me as a pathetic drunk. Grow a pair and I might stick around," Clarice challenged.

"Don't mince words, do you?"

"Something my late husband taught me. Doesn't pay to mollycoddle clients and encourage their pity parties."

"When did your husband pass away?"

"Disappeared. Not passed away."

"Sorry. You said 'late' husband. Just assumed."

"Easier that way. Too much to explain otherwise."

"Yet, you didn't say, took off, for instance. You said disappeared. Like, Harold Holt type, disappeared?"

"Not exactly..." she ventured without explanation.

"You brought it up. How long ago?"

Clarice thought carefully about whether or not to divulge the truth in answer to his question. It brought up such sad memories for her, and she wasn't sure if the answer would freak out the man in front of her even more. In the end, she relented.

"Six years," she almost whispered.

"Oh," he said, while Clarice examined his face for the connection.

"The same number of years you've been having problems here."

"That's a coincidence," remarked Graham without enthusiasm or interest.

"More than you know," she replied quietly.

"Oh?"

"Mr Bellows, my husband spent a portion of his youth here."

"In Tannum Sands?"

"Uh-huh."

"Whereabouts?"

"Here."

"Eh?"

"Here, in this house."

"Bullshit!"

"I can prove it."

"You gotta be shitting me?"

"I am shitting you not. My husband, Arlon Grey, grew up here for a few years before his parents moved to Brisbane with him. He would tell me snippets about his life here. Not with affection, mind you. He didn't have a happy childhood...or adulthood, for that matter."

"How come?"

"He was on the spectrum. A very rare form of autism that prevented him from exhibiting or understanding emotions. Most people he came into contact with thought he was either a freak or an arsehole."

"Yet you married him?"

"I did," she replied wistfully.

"You miss him?"

"Very, very much."

The silence stretched out uncomfortably.

"Any connection?" asked Graham.

"What do you mean?"

"You brought it up. You must think there's some sort of correlation between the time of your husband's disappearance and the events happening here?"

"My daughter would have you believe that. Me? I'm not convinced."

"Then why bring it up?"

"In the context of full disclosure."

"Can't be just that. I might be hungover but I saw the look you two exchanged when you saw the wall this morning. Something else there?"

"Maybe."

"What?"

"Are you sure you want to know?"

"No. Tell me anyway...'in the context of full disclosure'."

"I recognised the writing style of the word scrawled over our names. So did Tara. She wanted to say something about it but I stopped her."

"I don't understand. What do you mean, you recognised the style?"

"It was handwritten. I recognised the hand that wrote it."

"You know who's doing all this?"

"I didn't say that. I have no idea about what or who wrote our names on your wall. I did, however, immediately recognise the writing style of my husband when I saw the other word."

"How is that possible?"

"If you're asking me how my husband's handwriting appeared on that wall, I can't answer you. My daughter would probably say it was her father communicating with us from..."

Clarice couldn't finish the sentence. She only half-believed where he'd supposedly gone. She didn't think she could ever convince herself to accept Tara's explanation. Although she had witnessed her husband's disappearance, she had never spoken out loud about what might have happened or where he might have gone.

"From?"

"Pardon?"

"Where does your daughter think her father is communicating from?"

"You wouldn't believe me if I told you," admitted Clarice.

"From...the other side? Is that what she thinks? Does she think he might be the ghost haunting this place? For the six years, you said, since he'd been gone?"

"No. She doesn't. Not a ghost."

"What then?"

"I'm not going to go into it and I don't want you to raise the issue with her. I'm here to investigate this matter and she's only my assistant. If you can't accept that, we'll go and I'll return your money."

"Can you solve it? Can you make it stop?"

"I don't know."

"You could have lied."

"My name is Clarice Grey, wife of Arlon Grey, if he's still alive out there somewhere. I won't lie to you. I won't give you false hope. The only thing I can promise is that I'll do my best."

"Your husband was the detective, wasn't he?"

"Six years ago, yes. Now I am," said Clarice with a tone of steely determination.

CHAPTER SIX

Clarice joined Tara at the beach as the sun peered through the thinning clouds, casting a welcoming warmth upon the scene. The pair walked along the beach towards the main part of town in companionable silence. Clarice was waiting for her daughter to voice her observations. The secret smile playing on Tara's lips had not escaped Clarice's attention. She worried about that, feeling her daughter was heading for a great disappointment.

Tara surprised her by taking her hand. The bond she shared with her daughter had grown over the years since her adoption, a bond of such strength that it made Clarice's heart soar at times. Yet, for all the love and friendship they shared, it didn't come close to the relationship Tara had formed with Arlon Grey in the short time they were together, as impossible as it was to imagine that.

Clarice had to restrain herself from thoughts along those lines at times. Had she not also formed a very close relationship with the enigmatic man, the man who was incapable of love, incapable of friendship, emotions and feeling? She had loved...still loved him deeply. She knew in her heart that she could never find a man to replace Arlon Grey in her life, despite the desolation she had experienced when he disappeared...literally before her eyes.

One minute they were all gathered together in the middle of a freezing night in a temperate rainforest in Victoria, the next he... had dissolved into the night in a flash of blue and white light. She still thought it so...impossible. Despite the ordeal they had all experienced on an island where they first came across the phenomenon, she still couldn't accept her observations.

She knew Tara believed that her father had entered the other dimension he was subjected to when he interacted with the remnants of an ancient meteorite. Her young mind, around ten at the time he vanished, brooked no other possibility. She also knew, without a shadow of a doubt, that her father was unable to prevent it from happening. She believed that he would have moved heaven and earth to prevent their separation if there were even the slightest chance of him doing so.

Tara cried when it happened, but never afterwards. Her revelations about him being in her dreams, advising her, even assisting her, came as quite a shock to Clarice. Had she been entirely honest with her daughter or herself, though, she would have admitted to similar feelings and encounters in her troubling dreams.

The writing on the wall in Arlon Grey's distinctive hand dredged up more emotions and memories than she wished to deal with at present. She'd handled countless memos and reports from him over the years of her employment, and then her partnership with Arlon Grey, not to recognise his handwriting. It slapped her in the face the second she'd spied it. She had desperately hoped to hide her shock from Tara, but knew she'd failed.

"Are you going to wait all day before you say it?" asked Clarice gently.

"Daddy wrote it, didn't he?" asked Tara without requiring an answer, face full of eagerness and hope.

Clarice took in the stunning features of her adopted daughter, so vivacious and pure, happy, it seemed.

"Yes," she answered simply.

"You think it was meant for us?"

"Yes," said Clarice, studying her daughter's features as they stopped walking to face each other.

"Why?"

"Why do I think it was meant for us?"

"No, Mum. Why do you think he wants us to leave?"

"You expect me to answer that?"

"I guess not," said Tara sadly, turning to resume their walk.

"I hate to see you get your hopes up," said Clarice.

"You know how I feel about this. It isn't a coincidence and neither was that clap of thunder last night."

"What do you mean?"

"You know what I mean, Mum. It was the same as...you know?"

"Possibly."

"No way can you see it as anything else," Tara insisted, stopping to bury her bare feet in the wet sand as the gentle waves washed over them.

"We did have a storm last night, Tara," said Clarice, joining her to stare at the open ocean before them.

"Yeah, after! Anything on the equipment?"

"Nothing. The power went out, in case you missed that bit."

"Nothing registered or recorded before that?"

"Nope."

"What's next?"

"I want to poke around and ask some questions of the neighbours and the community in general. See if anyone else is experiencing anything out of the ordinary or can shed some light on the relationships in that family. I also want to talk to his wife and daughter alone, if I can swing it. You up for a trip to Gladstone?"

"I'll stick around here if that's okay?" answered Tara with a hint of mystery.

"Tara?" said her mum with a knowing glare.

"What?"

"Don't you 'what' me, young lady. What gives?"

"Well..."

"Hmm?"

"I might be meeting up with someone later on."

"What?" asked Clarice, showing signs of near panic, roughly turning Tara to face her.

"Mum, you're hurting me! I met someone swimming and we sorta made plans to meet up later on."

"Who?"

"Like you'd know him or something?"

"Him? Did you say..."

"Yes, Mum, him. I met a boy while I was swimming. He asked

if I'd like to meet him for a milkshake this afternoon."

"How old? What's he like? What was he wearing?...""

"Jeez, don't have a cow, Mum. He's my age, and what does it matter what he was wearing?"

"Well, if he wasn't wearing anything I *would* be 'having a cow'!"

"As if! We aren't at a nudist beach, Mum. He was wearing boardies, surfing after winning his iron man event for his age group in the nipper carnival, when he almost collected me. That's how we met."

"Harrumph! A surfie!"

"Wow. Way to socially profile someone, Mum. What's gotten into you? I have seen boys before. Remember? Sweet sixteen and *have* been kissed?"

"He kissed you?"

"Mum! Enough with the third degree, already."

"Just tell me if he tried to kiss you," Clarice demanded.

"I've only just met him. I'm not a slut, Mum."

Tara walked off in a huff. Clarice had to run to catch up.

"Sorry, Tara. I never meant to imply that you were. You just took me by surprise, that's all. I thought you wanted to help me investigate?"

"Nothing happens during the day as far as I can tell, and you want to go off to interview people. I'll just get in the way and possibly distract them from telling you what you might want to know."

"What do you mean?"

"Well, they might not open up to you with a kid in tow, even if I am sixteen."

"I still don't understand what..."

"Jeez, and you call yourself a detective. Sex stuff, Mum. They might not tell you the juicy bits about the Bellows if they see a kid around."

"Oh. I guess."

"Don't you want me making friends?"

"Sure I do, just the same gender is what I had in mind."

"You want me to be a lesbian?"

"Tara! Of course not!"

"Why not? What's wrong with being a lesbian?"

"Well, nothing. I..."

Tara snickered and Clarice knew she'd been suckered. She smiled. Tara was right to be indignant about the questioning. She had to trust her daughter to know right from wrong and to find her way around boys. Every girl had to make decisions like that eventually. Clarice had lost her virginity relatively late, but not everyone was as unlucky as she had been not to have the right sort of boys asking her out.

She sighed, knowing her love life was a thing of the past. She wasn't interested in finding anyone to replace Arlon. Her heart would always belong to him alone. That didn't mean she should stifle the life of her daughter, who was officially old enough to participate in sexual relations. Who knew if Tara remained a virgin? She wouldn't be the first girl to lie about something like that to her mother.

Clarice quickly dismissed that train of thought, fearing the answer. Tara and she maintained a healthy, honest relationship with each other based on trust and respect. She'd never had to resort to physical punishments where her daughter was concerned, abhorred the practice and condemned it in others.

She had once filmed a woman with her mobile phone when she witnessed her abusing her child in a park while Tara was playing on the swings. It was the closest she had ever come to instigating a physical fight. It took all of Clarice's strength to control her emotions enough to walk up to the abusive mother and show her the recording.

The youngish woman, with more piercings and tattoos than Clarice thought possible, dropped her three-year-old to the ground and lunged for the phone. It wasn't difficult for Clarice to subdue the woman in a chokehold she'd learned and countered often when her older brothers employed the tactic on her as a youngster. Growing up with five older brothers and a sister who didn't hold back in a stoush, soon gave Clarice all the ability she required to fend off most attackers.

She explained to the woman with the foul breath, spewing her vile language loud enough to cause all the other mothers to leave the area, that she had only two choices. Either she gave herself up to the police, and begged them to find her help to change her ways, or Clarice would take them the footage and she would be arrested and tried as a criminal. Although the woman continued to struggle, she slowed considerably as the threat sank in. Clarice guessed correctly that the woman was a single mother with few relatives capable of caring for her child if she went to jail.

When the woman finally nodded her acceptance of Clarice's ultimatum, she was allowed to break free. She grabbed her child roughly from the ground, where it was still crying miserably after being dumped. With a swagger and a middle finger salute, she marched out of the park.

Clarice followed her clandestinely for two weeks, collecting every piece of information she could gather. Her dossier on the woman was complete when she witnessed another incident of abuse. She gave the police all the information and the recordings of the two incidents she had captured on her smartphone. The child was placed into foster care while the mother was sent to prison. Bail was granted, but she was refused access to her child. A year later she was found guilty on all charges and imprisoned for eighteen months.

Clarice still felt guilty for stripping a mother of her child, and vice versa. She didn't regret her actions, fearing the child would eventually have suffered further and probably greater harm, but it niggled regardless.

Clarice became a single mother to ten-year-old Tara when Arlon disappeared and left her holding the reins of the company as well as the child. Tara had surely tested her mother's patience at times, as all children are prone to do. However, Clarice had never been driven to do more than send her daughter to bed early a couple of times, after explaining what she had done wrong. That was always *after* a meal; her daughter never went to bed hungry. Clarice considered herself extremely lucky. Tara was generally a well-behaved girl who responded to Clarice positively, usually accepting that her rare indiscretions warranted the punishment prescribed.

"So surfy-dude has a name?"

"No, his parents never felt like naming him. They settled for pointing at him and grunting something unintelligible most of the time."

"Smart-arse!"

"You swore."

"You haven't heard anything yet. If you ever see me and my brothers wrestling you'll hear language from me that will turn your hair white," said Clarice with a grin.

"His name is Doug Beech. Like the tree, not the sand," said Tara, pre-empting her mother's response.

"Was that how he explained it when you made the obvious comment about it being an appropriate name for him?"

"Yep," Tara agreed with a smile.

"Cute?"

"Hot!"

"I would have preferred cute or even handsome," Clarice said with a sigh.

"No one my age uses those words to describe a bloke anymore, Mum. Get with the program."

"My little girl, all grown up."

"You aren't rid of me yet. Still a few college years to go after high school."

"Any ideas what you want to do yet?"

"I've only ever wanted the one thing."

"What? Since when? This is the first time you've mentioned it," exclaimed Clarice. "What is that one thing you've only ever wanted?"

"To be a dick, like Daddy."

"Tara Blaze-Grey! How could you insult your..."

"Dick as in detective, Mum. I want to join the police force and become a detective like Daddy."

"It's not bad enough I have five brothers in the AFP risking their lives every day? I have to worry about my daughter as well?"

"What can I say? You asked. It can be the start of a long family tradition," suggested Tara with a shrug.

"Tara, you have a fortune coming your way in a couple of years. You can be anything you want, go anywhere, do anything, without ever having to work a day in your life. Don't get me wrong. I applaud the fact that you want a job, a career. I just can't understand your choice."

Tara took her time with her reply as they walked. She formulated the words in her mind before committing to them. She didn't want to come over as judgmental or accusatory. Clarice seemed to intuit her daughter's need to take a moment. For that, Tara was grateful.

"I'm not sure how to say this without it coming out wrong, Mum, without upsetting you."

"Well, by the way you're hesitating, I can only assume you will probably upset me, regardless of how tactful you want to be. So, best to rip the Band-Aid off in one go, eh?"

"Okay, but just remember, you asked me to do it this way."

"Go on, shock me."

"Unlike you, I want to use the skills I learn to find him."

"You...you *blame* me for his disappearance?" asked Clarice in astonishment.

"No. I blame you for not *looking* for him. You never tried to find him, never investigated his disappearance. I lost my daddy and you did nothing at all to bring him back to me," said Tara with tears in her eyes.

Riven to the core by her daughter's accusation left Clarice

reeling, suffering a kind of vertigo. Observing Tara's tears for her loss, for perhaps the first time, only accentuated the guilt and hurt Clarice suffered. She staggered with the weight of it, slowly descending to the soft sand, where she sat, immobile, hanging her head in shame and sadness.

"What could I do? How could I have begun looking...?" she asked in a whisper, shaking her head with renewed grief. "I lost my husband, the only man I've ever loved. He went...I don't know. You say to another dimension. How on earth do I find him there?"

"I'm sorry, Mummy. I shouldn't have said anything."

"No, no, I asked for it and you gave it. Both bloody barrels, straight to the heart. I never knew you felt so strongly about it. It's just, well...like trying to find the spirit of a dead person. How could I begin to..."

"It's not that. It's the fact that you never tried that I resent. You accepted that he was gone and that was the end of it. We didn't even go back to the island."

"The island?" Clarice asked in a confused haze.

"Well, that was where it all started. He might have ended up there, for all we know. It wouldn't have hurt to look, is all I'm saying. But you didn't. You just accepted it. Well, I can't. I won't accept that he's gone forever. I will spend the rest of my life, if necessary, dedicated to investigating his disappearance. I'll learn the craft, I'll buy the instruments, I'll follow the leads, anything I have to do to find him. I'll use my wealth in any way I can to find Arlon Grey," said Tara with an air of finality.

"You...you don't even know if he's still..."

"Yes, I do. He's alive, and I'll find him."

"How can you know?"

"That island episode bonded us in so many ways I can't begin to count them. I feel him. We were infused together by that force, made one in spirit and mind for a short time. I still have part of that connection. I still sense his life force out there, waiting for me to bring him home to us, to me."

Tara's strong words vibrated within Clarice. The determination and strength exhibited by her daughter made her feel inadequate. She would never have guessed that her daughter, whom she had raised alone and believed she had bonded with, could level such an accusation at her, such guilt.

"I never stopped loving him," she said eventually.

"I didn't question that, only your resolve, your duty to find him," admitted Tara as she went to sit by her mother on the damp sand, placing a comforting arm around her shaking shoulders. The clouds had gathered again overhead, cooling the air.

Clarice stared out to sea with a vacant expression. Her heart ached, for the man she loved and lost, for the daughter she had nurtured for years, only to find out she was resented by her. Clarice was appalled that Tara believed she didn't care enough or love her husband enough to investigate. There was simply nothing to scrutinise, in her opinion. How did one begin a search of another dimension? How did one begin to investigate a disappearance that had occurred before their eyes? How did one gather evidence when there wasn't a shred of it to be found, not in their reality, at any rate? How did one examine an empty space previously occupied by Arlon Grey?

"Sorry, Mum. I didn't mean to come over as angrily as that."

"I...I guess I... Shit, what a mess!"

"It's not as bad as that," assured Tara.

"I guess I deserved it. It could have been viewed that I did nothing whatever to search for my husband. I didn't. You're right," she admitted with a sigh. "He disappeared before our eyes and it never occurred to me to look for him. You were also right in that I blamed him for leaving us...me. I was furious with him. Took me a long time to get past that anger. Then the sorrow began. Oh, Tara, I'm so, so sorry, love. Arlon Grey would have left no stone unturned if the roles had been reversed. He'd have found me no matter where I ended up."

"Mum, don't..."

"Oh, I didn't think I would have had any sort of a chance at finding him, Tara. But I didn't try. It hurt like crazy to hear you say it, but you're right. I failed him...and you. I neglected the one thing I could do as an equal partner in the Bizarre and Mysterious Detective Agency: to mount an investigation. Couldn't get any more appropriate circumstances to engage our services than that, could we?" Clarice offered a wan smile.

Tara hugged her adopted mother warmly, knowing she had overstepped the line in her revelations. Clarice Grey-nee-Manning did not deserve to be put through the wringer by her daughter, who worshipped her parents. She remembered all too well the indifference and often open hostility exhibited by her natural parents.

She couldn't be entirely distraught about it, though. Had it not been for the series of events that had marooned her on Cid Island in the Whitsunday group all those years ago, she would not have come to know and cherish Clarice or Arlon Grey, especially Arlon. He was a cult hero, legend and super idol all rolled into one for Tara. His quirkiness and oddness never ceased to amaze and endear the man to her.

While almost everyone else baulked at the man, his mannerisms and his total lack of emotions, she thought him the most lovable man on earth for some reason that escaped both her and Clarice. She had hinted to her mother that it had something to do with the unique bonding they'd experienced, the coalition of minds that had occurred as a result of the foreign influence they'd encountered. It was only partially true. Tara had bonded immediately with the strange man the moment he rescued her and her biological mother.

He had spoken to her as no one ever had, or would again. He'd invested her with hope and solace at a time of great sorrow and danger. She had connected with him on multiple levels: as a fellow victim, as a survivor, as a realist. She was only nine at the time, yet she'd developed a deep and abiding relationship with the man long before events transpired to allow them to share a mental link.

Tara gazed out to sea longingly, wishing they could be back on that island, that she could once again be a child in his loving arms. The sense of security he provided was immeasurable and missed by her every day. She wondered what he might be doing, wherever he was.

CHAPTER SEVEN

GO AWAY read the new message over the top of the names the following morning, in the same hand as previously.

Apart from the air-rending crack of thunder-that-wasn't-thunder, nothing else of note had occurred the night before: no odd glunking sounds, no electricity interruption, nothing else untoward. As on the previous night, Clarice's equipment didn't record anything: not on tape, video or thermal scan, nothing.

"So your husband has to be dead," stated Graham.

"I've already explained that he isn't," said Clarice.

"Well, he has to be if he's the ghost writing that on the wall, doesn't he? Why would he be telling you to bugger off?"

"He is not dead!" Tara roared, rising from the breakfast table.

"That's enough, Tara. No need for that. I'm sure Graham meant no offence?" she inquired of the man with a nod of encouragement.

"No, none at all. Sorry if you took it that way. Just trying to make sense of things," he said in a haggard manner denoting his weariness.

"My husband...disappeared, Mr Bellows. Neither Tara nor I truly believe he passed away. I don't know how this ties into what's happening here yet; it's too early to say. It may be all just a big coincidence."

"You can't believe that, Mum?" cried Tara.

"You have to forgive my daughter and *assistant*," said Clarice, with great emphasis on the last word, glowering at Tara. "She has always believed her father would try to reach her from wherever he went."

"Why wouldn't he be able to reach you if he wanted to? Not to sound offensive or anything, but aren't you in a bit of denial? If he left you..."

"He didn't leave us," said Clarice quietly. "He would never

have left us intentionally," she whispered to Tara, who nodded in agreement.

Tara and Clarice had grown closer through the emotionally-charged experiences the previous day. Clarice had come to accept much of what her daughter said, admitting to herself that she was wrong in many respects when it came to her inaction after it all happened.

"He hasn't died and he hasn't left you. You say he's disappeared. I may be just a common shop clerk, but that doesn't make much sense to me, and I'm paying you to make some sense."

Clarice sighed, knowing an explanation of sorts was warranted. She wasn't prepared, wasn't sure where to begin with something she had barely believed possible for six years. Her eyes strayed to Tara, who had resumed her seat. She nodded at her mum to continue.

"Mr Bellows, do you accept that what's occurring here is beyond conventional explanation?"

"Called *you*, didn't I?" he asked sullenly.

"Fair comment. Seven years ago, I talked Arlon Grey into helping my sister, whose husband had died in very peculiar circumstances. We were newly engaged and I thought the case would give us a chance to cement our relationship, because we would be spending time together on an island in the Whitsunday group.

"During our investigations, we managed to rescue this beautiful young girl, who ended up losing both her parents in the tragedy. My husband was subjected to a foreign energy source from an ancient meteorite originating from an asteroid we believe crossed through not only space, but dimensions, which affected him on a molecular level. It still pains me to think about it.

"A year later, we were investigating a case in Victoria, when Arlon began exhibiting signs of abnormal behaviour in relation to that energy. He practically glowed with a bright blue aura. It continued to increase in intensity until he vanished before our eyes into that blueish/white haze," Clarice finished with tears falling freely.

Tara rose to offer some comfort.

"Where to?"

"To another dimension," Tara answered before her mother could evade the truth.

"Another...dimension?" questioned Graham with growing scorn.

"Huh, you're perfectly willing to accept displaced spirits, wandering souls in the afterlife, but not the possibility of other dimensions?"

"That's enough, Tara. Apologise immediately and hold your tongue. I will not have you insulting our client, regardless of your strong beliefs," Clarice warned her.

Tara took in the pose and the intonation and backed away. She returned to her seat to finish her breakfast of cereal.

"Sorry, Mr Bellows," she said with a half-full mouth.

"Thank you, but you're right to be angry with me. I shouldn't be sceptical of anything at this point. I'm the one that called you guys in. I haven't found any reasonable explanation for what's been happening and it's torn me and my family apart. I guess I was stunned by the revelation that it might have something to do with your father. I apologise as well. Mrs Grey...?"

"Clarice will be fine."

"Clarice, tell me more about the dimension-thing. I'd like to know," he asked with sincerity.

"I can't adequately explain the scientific intricacies of it all. Arlon found out from an old fisherman that a meteorite had created a deep bay on the island we were investigating. The meteorite had broken in two, with the halves ending up some distance from each other at opposite ends of the bay. My sister and her husband found the two pieces and transported them back to their house to decorate a path, bringing them into proximity to one another again. That proximity caused the halves to react in a detrimental manner that ultimately caused the death of my brother-in-law. It also produced phenomena that Arlon Grey believed to be portals to another dimension, the one where the asteroid originated.

"When Arlon reunited the fragments it caused a near cataclysmic event. It also profoundly affected my husband, causing him to hear thoughts, communicate telepathically, emanate aural energy and even heal people. Unfortunately, the more he used that energy the stronger it became, until it finally took him altogether."

"Six years ago?" he asked.

"Six long, lonely years ago," Clarice agreed sadly.

"Do you mind if I ask what your daughter thinks?"

"Go ahead," answered Clarice after a moment's reflection.

They were both looking at Tara; she paused mid-spoon.

"I'd better not," she said finally.

"Go ahead, Tara. You opened this can of worms, now help us digest them," urged Clarice.

"Eew! Not while I'm eating, Mum!"

"Go on, Tara."

"I...don't think I ever lost contact with Daddy...up here," she said, pointing to her head. "I see and hear him in my dreams and when I'm awake sometimes. I know this has something to do with him coming back to us...to me."

"There you have it," said Clarice with a note of finality, fearing the end of the contract.

Graham took his time to mull over the information. He nodded his head and shook it alternately as he weighed up all the pros and cons.

Finally, he said, "I'm out of my league here. It took me months to get up the courage to call you, suspecting I would be received as a total fruitcake once I revealed my problem. If I hadn't seen the physical manifestations of these nightly visits and my family were not affected by them, I wouldn't have bothered. I don't believe this guff, yet I have no choice, because it's happening. I've seen the proof. The fact that the other writing showed up the day you arrived lends weight to your story, young lady. Not sure that I can completely accept *everything*. It's just so far out of my comfort zone that my mind refuses to accept it. I'll try to keep an open mind going forward. I need a conclusion to all this. My family and I are depending on you two to put an end to it, one way or the other.

"I don't want to lose this house where my daughter was born, but I won't risk the lives of the two people I love more in the world than anything else. Clarice, how do you see this playing out?"

"For what it's worth, I see an escalation because of our presence. When you first mentioned it, I also thought immediately of an attempt by my husband to reach us. More wishful thinking than anything else?" she shrugged at Tara. "I don't know what the handwriting over the top of our names signifies at this point. That it is in Arlon's hand makes it somewhat clear that he wants us to leave, yet the names underneath seem to mean the opposite."

"He's trying to protect us," blurted Tara.

"From what?" asked Graham and Clarice together.

"From whoever wrote our names on the wall."

"And you know this because...?" asked Clarice.

"Pretty obvious, isn't it?"

"Not to me, young lady. Nor, I suspect, to Graham."

"He doesn't want us near here when it happens."

"When what happens?"

"I dunno."

"That would be...I don't know, Tara. Not 'dunno'."

"Sorry, Mum."

"What do you *think* might happen?" asked Graham.

"Something bad. Daddy is trying to protect us by sending us away. That's all I know."

"How do you know this, Tara?" asked Clarice with growing concern. Noting her daughter's reluctance to answer, she persisted. "Tara?"

Sighing, she answered, "He told me."

"Who told you what and when?" asked Clarice in alarm.

"Daddy. He told me in a dream last night."

"Your father told you that we should go away in a dream last night?"

"No, he didn't speak, really. He was sort of...pushing me away with his mind. I felt the urge to go this morning when I woke up."

"First you say you feel the urge to be here, even sneaking out of your room to hitch a ride here in the middle of the night. Now you say you want to go?"

"I didn't say that. I don't want to go. I just felt the urge to leave. Daddy was trying hard to get me to go, to protect me...and you."

"This is getting weirder by the minute," said Graham, with his head in his hands.

"I don't know what to tell you, Graham. My daughter is not in the habit of lying, but I feel much the same way as you do. I find it difficult to accept her revelations."

"Mum!"

"Well, it's true, pet."

"Thanks a lot." Tara stormed out of the kitchen and the house.

"I'm sorry about that, Graham."

"Nothing to be sorry for. Will she be all right?"

"I imagine so. She needs a little time. I didn't want to bring her along for just these reasons. She misses her dad far more than she will ever admit. I always suspected that she hid her feelings about him to protect me. Turns out she believes she has been in contact with Arlon the whole time, only she can't define the exact conversation or moment it takes place other than vague references to dreams."

"Is she...you know?"

"What?"

" All right in the head?"

"Is she having a mental episode that could be defined as abnormal? Is that what you're asking me, her mother?" said Clarice with a steely glare.

"I guess not. Sorry."

Clarice went outside to check on Tara, but she was nowhere to be found. Finding the caravan empty as well, Clarice assumed that Tara had either gone to the beach or connected with the young lad, Doug...something-or-other. Beach! Clarice reminded herself. No, not Beach like the sand, but Beech like the tree, she corrected.

Clarice did not follow her daughter. She still had some neighbours to interview, and Graham's wife and daughter would be arriving later in the day. She wanted to get their testimony before they headed back to Gladstone again. Graham, understandably, did not want his wife and daughter to stay the night. It was bad enough that he had to stay, he'd said.

Clarice had found one piece of puzzling evidence, outside one of the windows to the lounge room, on her earlier examination of the house and grounds. She was reasonably confident it had not been there the day before. Below the window was a patch of ground with only a few blades of grass peering through the sandy soil. A clear, deep footprint was outlined in the soft ground, indicating a large and heavy person had stood there.

Clarice first considered it nothing more onerous than a peeping Tom. She changed her opinion when she thought how unlikely it would be to have multiple unconnected events occurring. It had to be related to the manifestations, she concluded. Other than the size, which was very large, the queer aspect of the print was the talon-like punctures at the end of the toes: five neat conical holes at the end of each digital imprint. But the truly odd thing about the print was that it faced away from the window. It was as though someone had exited the house by jumping from the window, making a deep impression below.

Clarice scoured the area for further impressions or signs of disturbance without success...until she examined the wall beneath the window carefully. The paintwork, such as it was, due to recent neglect, was scratched. That married with the print to a certain extent, if one imagined a person exiting through the window, having to grab onto the sill, especially if quite a large person had manoeuvred themselves out of a tiny frame.

It didn't explain why the person was barefoot, or the punctures at the end of the toes. Clarice would have to make a plaster cast and take photos to send to her contact in forensics. Thanks to her brothers in the AFP, Clarice had many contacts on whom she could depend. She walked to the caravan to retrieve her equipment and saw Tara returning.

"I forgot to ask how it went with the sand boy?"

"Sand boy?"

"Beach...sand?"

"That's so lame," Tara said of Clarice's attempt at humour.

"I know his name is Doug, don't get in a huff."

"How come you didn't ask me about him last night? You were so worked up about him yesterday that I thought I would get the third degree."

"Gave you some space to talk about it yourself. That didn't work," Clarice commented, as she proceeded to gather the equipment she required.

"What're you up to?"

"Making a cast of a footprint."

"You found a print? Where?"

"In the ground."

"Oh, you're a barrel of laughs today, aren't you? Thinking of a career change? I wouldn't quit your day job just yet," said Tara with a smirk.

"Stop changing the subject. How'd it go?"

"Nothing special. We just had milkshakes at the cafe, talked a bit and then we split."

"Did he ask for your number?"

"Yeah."

"And?"

"I didn't give it to him. I asked for his instead."

"Clever girl. Going to contact him?"

"Probably."

"Listen, about this morning..."

"No, I understand," said Tara, following her mother around the house, helping her to carry some gear. "You couldn't know how I felt about Daddy, and that's okay. I don't need you to. All I need is that you allow me to believe what I believe."

"That is very mature of you, Tara."

"Wow, that's a big dude," exclaimed Tara when she spied the print. "That's twice the size of my foot. "Is it even human?"

"What do you think?" asked Clarice, as she prepared for the cast by mixing the plaster with water from a garden hose in a bucket.

"Fairly slim, I would have thought, for someone that large, and what's with the holes in front?"

"Good question. Have an answer?"

" Bloody long toenails?"

"Tara!"

"What?"

"Swearing is what."

"Come on, Mum. 'Bloody' doesn't qualify as swearing in Australia. Not like I dropped the F-bomb or anything."

"Still."

"Jeez!"

"Help me with this, would you? I *am* paying you to assist me, remember?"

"First I heard of it. You mean real wages?"

"More like a performance-based reimbursement."

"You hadn't brought it up before now."

"I figured I would pay you what I thought you were worth. So far, I haven't witnessed much assisting, only social outings."

"You told me to go to the beach," Tara defended herself.

"To the beach, I said. Not a beach person."

"Jokes again?"

"Sort of. Not funny?"

"Not even a little bit."

"Harsh!"

They both laughed. Mother and daughter were back on track

with each other. They completed their task in companionable silence.

"Make any observations while we did that?" asked Clarice, when they were back at the van inspecting the odd cast.

"Like the size and the narrowness, you mean?" asked Tara after a moment's reflection.

"No."

"Can you give me a hint?"

"You want to be a detective, yet aren't willing to use your powers of observation and deduction? Think," Clarice instructed. "Use your mind to picture the print beneath the window and take it all in. Question everything about it and its relevance to the investigation as well as the positioning."

"You think it was someone spying on us?"

"Do I?"

"Ooh, that could get annoying."

"I don't want to provide the answers *I've* arrived at. They may not even be accurate. I want to use you as a sounding board and see if you can come up with your own set of observations and conclusions. Think it through logically, Tara, from beginning to end. Build a possible scenario, a set of circumstances around the print, to conclude how it might have appeared there."

"Well, it's obvious that someone, a large someone, was looking through that window at us, last night, presumably, because you would have told me if you'd found the print before today."

Clarice nodded. Then she smiled when Tara's face screwed up with disgust at herself.

"Bugger! How could someone be looking through the window and leave a print facing away from it!"

"Exactly."

"So someone was leaving through the window? They jumped down, making a deeper impression than normal."

"Pretty good."

"Not good! Not good by a bloody long shot! That barefoot

pervert was in the house, possibly while we were in there?"

"Stop the language, young lady. I won't be telling you again."

"Mum..."

"Tara, I don't want you getting in the habit of swearing, even mildly. I realise it's not as bad as some, but it still gets to be a bad habit if you keep resorting to it. Pretty soon you'll be throwing out F-bombs and worse. I wouldn't like to be in your shoes if I catch you."

"Mum, that's scary, knowing someone was in the house."

"I don't know about that. I'm happier with someone real being in there."

"I thought you got off on all that paranormal guff?"

"I don't 'get off' on it, Tara Blaze-Grey..."

Tara was giggling so hard that Clarice was unable to finish.

"All right, Miss Smarty Pants. Care to explain how someone jumps out of a locked window? One that I locked personally with my hair alarm to inform me if it had been opened."

"Hair alarm?"

"A single strand of hair attached to the window and the sill. Almost impossible to see if you don't know what to look for. Well? A deeper than normal footprint, facing the street, beneath a locked window."

"I dunno...sorry. I *don't know* what that could mean. I do know I'm not going to like whatever explanation you're about to give me."

"Think it through logically and it can only really leave one conclusion," Clarice prompted.

Tara pondered the problem, screwing her face up in concentration. "The roof!" she exclaimed.

"That was what I came up with. I'm going to go up there and poke around, if Graham has a ladder I can use."

"What can you hope to find?"

"I won't know until I'm up there."

"You're pretty good at this, Mum. I had no idea."

"Who do you think has been keeping the business going all this time?"

"Oh, I guess I just thought you pretty-well muddled your way through," Tara confessed with a look of contrition.

"Well, thank you for the vote of confidence. 'Muddled my way through', indeed!"

"How do you know this stuff, then?"

"Mostly from your father. When we formed the new agency, he drilled the procedures into me and gave me quite a few tips. He always encouraged me to use my grey matter, and sought my opinion on everything we did. He was a very good teacher."

"Good role model as well. I don't think I've ever come across a more gentle and wise man. Yet he could fight better than most while never showing aggression."

"He couldn't. You know that."

"I miss him so much, Mum."

"I know. I do, too."

"I'm going to pick up my wife and daughter." Graham rounded the van, startling the pair. "What's that?" he asked, indicating the plaster cast Clarice was holding.

"Might be our mysterious author with the limited vocabulary," offered Clarice. "I made this from an imprint I found beneath the lounge room window."

"He was in the house?"

"Hard to say for sure. Someone had to be in the house at some point to leave our names there. They neither entered nor exited through that window, though, because I locked it and it stayed locked."

"So, no break-in then?"

"Not as far as I can tell."

"I'm feeling a bit relieved, strangely."

"Not so strange. I had similar thoughts just minutes ago. It makes you feel as though we are dealing with something more tangible than ghosts?"

"Yeah, that's it exactly."

"I hate to burst your bubble, but there is still someone getting inside the house, without triggering any of the electronic or physical traps, to write that stuff on the walls. I don't know too many persons able to do that. No heat signature, no sound activation or movement alarms, nothing. Not too many people can produce that thunder we heard, either," explained Clarice apologetically.

"Well, that was the storm, naturally."

"Nope, nothing natural about it. The thunder came before the storm hit. Did you recognise the sound, Tara?"

"Yeah...I mean, yes."

"Same as we've heard before, if you allow your mind to go there," suggested Clarice.

"The island."

"Exactly, just as you said."

"Mum? Are you trying to say there's another meteorite around here?"

"No, not at all. The odds of another one would be astronomical."

"Hardy, har, har," sneered Tara.

"What?"

"Astronomical?"

"Oh, I didn't mean that," said Clarice chuckling.

"What *do* you mean?" asked Graham with impatience.

"I mean that the sound being unconnected to a regular weather storm is similar to what we experienced on that island. That's all. I can't even begin to guess what that implies or how it affects us."

"I thought I was paying you to come up with answers, not guesses?"

"I detect a tone, Mr Bellows. It's been only two days. I don't think I ever gave the impression that an investigation of this or any other nature was quickly resolvable? Not in two days, at any rate. Look at you, you're a state! Do you really want to pick up your wife and daughter looking like that? No wonder they aren't hanging around. I wouldn't have enough confidence in a drunken father and husband to stay, either. Before you start throwing accusations of incompetence my way, I'd start looking at yourself."

Graham was silenced by Clarice's cold outburst. He turned slowly about and walked back to the house as if in a daze.

"Way to go, Mum," exclaimed Tara, when Graham was out of earshot.

"He needed a reality check," said Clarice without conviction.

"Psychologist now?"

"I have to wear many hats in this sort of business. Some clients need to be mollycoddled, some need encouragement, some need a firmer hand. That man is losing himself and soon won't be of benefit to anyone, let alone his family, who need him the most. His heavy drinking and despondency are hampering his usefulness to us and this situation."

"He's scared witless, Mum."

"I get that, I truly do. But fear can become a debilitating force that leaves no room for anything else, such as logic and strategy. He isn't thinking clearly any more. He's allowing the events to crush his spirit and his resolve. He's a beaten man and that will endanger himself, us and his family. I'm thinking of advising him not to bring them here."

"That could be worse for him, couldn't it?"

Clarice stared at her perceptive daughter for a few moments, considering her question. Julie and Cynthia Bellows were on their way from Gladstone on the bus, regardless of her wishes. They were due in the centre of town in half an hour. If she pushed, she might be able to convince Graham to make them get on the return bus. Despite her desire to interview the wife about her side of the events and to examine the girl, she did not want them subjected to what the man in their lives had become.

Graham had been hiding his drinking habits since being rebuked by Clarice and prohibited from excesses while the investigation proceeded. However, it didn't take a detective to smell the alcohol exuding from his pores and on his breath, despite all the mints he chewed. His bloodshot eyes and unsteadiness also indicated his reluctance to stop partaking from the moment he arose in the mornings.

After six years of repeated visitations and harm to himself and his family, it was understandable that the habit had taken root. His need to shield the hurt from himself and others had taken hold of him. Whether he had always had the propensity for alcohol addiction was not Clarice's concern. Her chief concern was the safety of her daughter and herself, followed by the safety and well-being of her clients.

It would always fall in that order as far as Clarice was concerned. She wasn't some sort of hero, ready to fall on her sword to protect others, and certainly never willing to risk the life of her daughter. She regretted bringing Tara along. Then she remembered that she had had little choice in that decision; Tara had forced her hand. It still rankled with her. Her daughter could be very obstinate at times. However, it was the first time Tara had shown a willingness to break the rules attempting something as dangerous as hitchhiking.

CHAPTER EIGHT

Julie Bellows possibly had been a stunning woman in her youth. She might have retained her attractiveness into her later years, but the trauma she and her family had faced for six years had taken their toll on her delicate features. She exhibited the same harrowed look and furrowed brow as her husband, perpetually creased in fear and concern.

Clarice barely topped the tape at one point five metres tall, yet she seemed to tower over the diminutive woman. Clarice did not make the mistake of underestimating her, however. It was clear from the outset that she possessed a will of iron when protecting her family, like a lioness with cubs. Her daughter, Cynthia, refused to leave her side.

The daughter was possibly only a few years younger than Tara, yet she had the mannerisms of someone much younger, unable to look anyone in the eyes and terrified to be apart from an adult. They both seemed to recoil from Graham's advances, endorsing Clarice's earlier observations of him.

They were crowded into the small kitchen, the adults drinking coffee, the teens, hot chocolate. Tara was trying her best to engage the girl in conversation, but without success. Clarice smiled at her when she looked up. The tension was palpable, the fear coming off the family unit in waves. Clarice's request to examine Cynthia was met with a blunt refusal.

"Mrs Bellows, I'm not quite sure I understand why you're here if you don't want to discuss the situation and you won't allow me to talk to or examine your daughter?"

"Are you a doctor?"

"Of course not," replied Clarice kindly.

"So why would you be interested in examining my daughter?"

"*Our* daughter, Julie."

Julie ignored her husband's remark, glaring straight at Clarice, waiting for an answer.

"I have no medical opinions to offer. I just wanted to see her injuries to better understand what we're dealing with here."

"Monsters," she declared without hesitation.

"Now, Julie..."

"Don't you patronise me, Graham Bellows. You may hide from our problems in a bottle, but don't expect the rest of us to shy from the truth," exclaimed Julie with a steely resolve.

Both mother and daughter had similar blonde bob cuts, bouncing around their heads as they nodded with certainty about Julie's statement.

"Monsters?" asked Clarice gently.

"Only my girl's seen them and that's good enough for me. Attacked her while she slept. Cynthia screaming night after night, getting cuts and bruises all over. Place should be demolished and start again, with us as far away as possible."

"How do you propose we accomplish that, dear?" asked Graham with a sneer.

"If you hadn't wasted all our savings on booze and this lot, we might have been gone by now...as a family," she stated emphatically.

"What's that mean?" asked Graham with growing concern.

"I only came back to gather what's left of our things, then we're off...for good."

"You can't..."

"Oh, and why might that be?"

"Cynthia..."

"Yeah, that's right, Cynthia. Your daughter. Remember her now, do you?"

"I never stopped..."

"Oh, don't start all that nonsense now, Graham Bellows. You stopped caring about her and me a long time ago. You'd rather find your love in a bottle than have the courage to face up to all this and protect us from what's been going on. Well, not me. You hear? I'll not stay here another day while you don't have a backbone in your body. You don't deserve our love and I will not see my daughter harmed any longer. You," she said, turning her attention to Clarice, "you're probably not a bad person, but I don't agree with what he done calling you in, selling off our assets. Shoulda called in a priest or something to exorcise the place."

"I'm sorry it happened that way, Mrs Bellows, I truly am," explained Clarice. "While I can't return all of it I can refund the remainder that hasn't been used."

"Too late for that now. Damage has been done and I wouldn't want him to have even more money to buy booze. No, I don't want the money back. I have an uncle in Melbourne who's agreed to take us in and even give me a job in his factory, making workwear. That's where me and the little one are going."

"You can't take my daughter away from me," said Graham in a painful whine.

"Listen to him, would you? Not an ounce of spunk in him. No fight, nothing. Just that horrible wheedling tone that could drive a woman to hate. I won't subject my daughter to that one day longer. I agreed to come back and, maybe, answer some questions for the lady and to get our things. Then we have a train ride to Melbourne, once we get back to Gladstone. If you ever find a backbone and stop wallowing in self-pity, you can visit your daughter. Until then, stay away and don't try calling. Don't even think about calling if you're still drinking. My uncle made it clear he'll protect us from you."

"Mrs Bellows, can I ask your daughter to possibly explain what she saw? Maybe give us some details about the...monsters, a description?"

"Go ahead, Cynthia, tell 'em," ordered her mother.

"Th-they come outta the blue, they do," said Cynthia in a shaky tone, fraught with reservations and chilling fear.

"You mean they appear randomly?" asked Clarice in the gentlest tone she could muster, wondering how such a young person had come across that term.

"Nuh. Outta the blue that happens to my wall. Sometimes it's just a head or an arm, sometimes half of it. Different walls. Once, one come outta my wall at the head of me bed and swiped at me with its claws, scratching my back as I tried to crawl away. It hurt so bad," said the girl in a whisper, shivering with dread.

"Can you describe it?"

"All grey skin. Like an elephant's, with wrinkles and...no hair. They make weird sounds that vibrate through me sometimes, making me sick. The mouths....so, so horrible..."

"That's enough. I don't want her any more scared than she is, poor thing. This has been an absolute nightmare for us, especially her. I haven't seen them and I don't want to. I trust my daughter when she says she saw them. Proof is in the deep scratches she suffered. No way could she have done that to herself, either, if that's what you were thinking and hoping to find out by examining her. You'll just have to take our word for it," said Julie with finality. Now if you'll..."

Julie stopped as they all heard the ominous sounds resonating about them.

Glunk, glunk, glunk.

It was a deep, throaty tone, reminiscent of the sound an emu makes, or so it seemed to Clarice. The vibrations could be felt thrumming through the floorboards and the chairs on which they sat. Cynthia's eyes were open wide in abject horror. Graham groaned, while Julie shook with fear and anger. Tara did not feel any fear, as far as her mother could tell. She seemed more curious about it than anything else.

Glunk, glunk, glunk.

The sounds were closer, louder and more onerous. A sudden, ear-splitting crack above their heads shocked them all to the core. The ceiling seemed to shimmer in pulsating waves, with flecks of blue appearing through the white paint. The lights flickered before dying, while the kitchen implements resting on the benchtops came alive on their own. The blender blended air. The toaster racks bobbed up and down. The coffee-maker gurgled as it tried to slurp up the remaining droplets of water in the overhead bowl.

The door to the fridge flew open suddenly, causing a milk carafe to topple to the floor, where it exploded into a million shards of dripping glass. The microwave oven began to ping persistently, as though it was urging the household to open the door and retrieve the cooked goods inside. The garbage unit in the sink whirred noisily, grinding away laboriously at nothing.

Cynthia's high-pitched screams added to the cacophony. Julie clutched her daughter in a protective embrace, rising with her from the chairs. Clarice was unable to determine a course of action that might alleviate the mother's concerns or her own. A glance at the recording materials in the hallway indicated no activity. Clarice watched as Julie moved slowly back towards a wall, eyes staring above and around her.

The radio atop the fridge suddenly blared out an old tune from the seventies, before landing on the floor in a shower of plastic and electronic components. The ceiling fan whirred faster and faster until it was simply a blur, causing strong down currents that pushed cups and saucers off the table below it. Cupboard doors opened and banged shut, their contents rattling and rotating until they were flung outwards, smashing to pieces against the walls.

The cutlery drawer shot out, catapulting all the pieces within from the interior tray to leave forks and knives twanging as they embedded themselves into the walls and ceiling. The occupants seated at the table dove under it the moment the cutlery began to slice through the room.

Glunk, glunk, glunk.

Louder and louder the noise became, increasing the level of discomfort it caused to the room's inhabitants. The deep base reverberations pounded through flesh and the senses to the bones within, making them vibrate and ache. To Clarice, it felt as though her marrow had melted and was sloshing about within her bones, causing a deep-seated throb to course through her entire body. She heard Tara crying out to her through the maelstrom, but couldn't make a move towards her. Her body was incapable of responding to her commands.

The walls began to undulate in regular waves. The house groaned in protest at the unnatural forces attacking its structure. Window panes popped and shattered in their frames. From her position under the table, Clarice saw Julie's and Cynthia's feet gradually backing up to a wall.

Assuming the cutlery had all been thrown, Clarice rose from under the table. All the kitchen appliances were still going ten to the dozen. The ceiling and walls had taken on a surreal movement, as though elements in a Salvador Dali painting. Clarice instinctively searched for a melting clock on the wall. Fortunately, no clock existed in the kitchen.

Graham and Tara had also risen from beneath the table, staring aghast at the mayhem about them. Julie and Cynthia clutched each other desperately against the wall; a faint bluish haze shimmered behind them.

Glunk, glunk, glunk.

The maddening sound continued to knife through their senses, causing their bones to quake and shiver. As Clarice winced with the pain of it, watching her daughter and Graham buckling under the pain it caused, she saw something coming through the wall directly behind and slightly above Julie's head.

The pale grey hand, with needle-sharp extrusions from the digits, grasped Julie's blonde hair, yanking her painfully backwards. Another ghostly hand appeared to the side of Julie's head. The end of a sharp finger pierced her neck.

As the commotion about them gradually abated, the group watched in horror as the hand grasping Julie's hair forced her head back through the wall, which had turned a brilliant, shimmering blue. Only Cynthia was unaware of the peril her mother faced. She became aware of the others staring in her direction. When she peered upwards to witness what they were looking at, she screamed again and fainted.

Clarice was the first to break out of the spell of inactivity to rush to Julie's aid. She grabbed one of the woman's hands, hauling back with all her might against the opposing force. Julie's screams had been cut short once her head disappeared into the wall.

"Don't just stand there, help me," Clarice shouted at Graham.

He stood rooted to the spot, unable to understand what was happening or how to respond. Tara moved instead, rushing to her mother's side, grabbing Julie's other flailing hand. The pair of them pulled with all their might, trying to stop her from being taken. However, the opposing force was beyond their abilities. Before they, too, could be sucked into the wall, they released Julie's hands simultaneously. She was flung through the wall easily once all resistance had ceased on their side.

Graham rushed to the laundry room, directly behind the kitchen wall through which his wife had disappeared. He returned a moment later, shaking his head.

Clarice and Tara had both moved to support Cynthia, who was gradually regaining her senses. As she remembered where she was, and the horrible fate that had befallen her mother, the young girl became hysterical. They did what they could to pacify and calm her.

The house took on an eerie silence once the girl settled into quiet sobs, comforted by Tara, who held her tight. Clarice watched as Graham circled the kitchen, taking in the devastation. He held his head with his hands as if to contain what might be trying to escape. He lurched sideways, veering towards the hallway and his bedroom beyond. Clarice knew where he was going and why. She didn't try to stop him. She didn't think she could or that it would be wise to attempt it.

Cynthia succumbed to emotional exhaustion, falling asleep in the caravan situated in the backyard. She could not be convinced to remain in the house, in her bedroom. Tara was watching over her, reading an ebook in the forward eating area. Clarice had searched the entire house and surrounds without success, finding no hint of Julie's whereabouts. Graham Bellows remained passed out in the main bedroom: at least he was the last time she checked on him.

The kitchen had been restored to a semblance of normality. Clarice sat at the kitchen table with a frown creasing her features, sipping silently from a cup of tea. She was no longer a regular tea drinker since marrying Arlon Grey, who was a coffee drinker through and through. The special local blends he purchased had won her over. After their ordeal earlier, she felt that relaxation was preferable to a caffeine high.

She had made a call to one of her brothers in the AFP, alerting him to possible abductions and...other incidents at the house. Despite witnessing events that had transpired on a case many years prior, her brother was reluctant to take on board the information she delivered. The local police were once more unimpressed with the latest developments at the troublesome location. They told Clarice to file a missing person's report after twenty-four hours had passed.

Clarice pondered the new message scrawled on the wall during the chaos.

Ɛ-G --ℛ-Ө-S SӨ--Ɗ --ӨӨ--Ӽ-

It was in the familiar and heart-breaking hand of her husband once more, but made no sense to her. The letters in between the ones she recognised were unintelligible: blurred beyond semblance of understanding. She had a pen and pad in front of her on which she'd been attempting to decipher the message. The only one she felt comfortable with was the first word, which she believed to contain only three letters, beginning with an 'E', and ending in a 'G'. She could find only three words to match it in her Scrabble dictionary, which she always kept handy: erg, a shortening of ergometer; eng, another name for agma, and egg. None of these held meaning or relevance, in Clarice's opinion.

She considered she might have read it wrongly, or that the author had miswritten something, such as placing a space where it shouldn't have been, lengthening the first word to more than three letters. In that case, she was truly stumped.

Clarice was gravely concerned for their safety; she was wrong to have brought Tara along. She was sorely tempted to remove themselves from the area, convinced that she had bitten off more than she could chew. There didn't seem to be anything she could do. Her recording equipment had finally captured the strange sounds that seemed to penetrate their bodies and set their bones vibrating, but failed to film anything. The writing had appeared on the wall as if by magic, with no names scrawled beneath it.

On impulse, she had taken a sample of the material from which the words had been written, also assuming it to be blood, and asked the lab to compare the samples to the last lot she'd sent. It would be interesting to ascertain if the names that appeared on the wall were written with the same blood type. She asked for a full DNA analysis. As an afterthought, she also asked if the police department kept a DNA record of their officers.

Tara wandered into the kitchen to join her mother.

"Still sleeping?" asked Clarice.

"Yeah, she's out like a light. Want me to go back out?"

"I think you can stay for a little while. Tea?"

"Since when do you drink tea?"

"I've had enough stimulation for one day, thank you. I made a pot, on the counter." Clarice pointed.

"I'm amazed you managed to straighten the mess. Cupboard doors are a bit warped," observed Tara as she went about making herself a cuppa.

"Do you need that much sugar, young lady?" asked Clarice, watching Tara heaping it into her cup.

"I just need something sweet and couldn't find any chocolate."

"And who said you could snavel my chocolate if I did have any?" Clarice teased.

Tara smiled and settled at the table opposite her mother with her brew.

"Did you bring any?"

"Me to know."

"I will find out, you know?"

"Put your detecting skills to the test, then, my dear."

A short silence ensued as both of them pursued their thoughts. Clarice peered at her daughter with warm affection. She wore skin-tight jeans and a plain black T-shirt, accentuating all her young curves to perfection. Tara had blossomed in the last couple of years into a lovely young lady. Clarice sighed inwardly, knowing she would be left alone soon while Tara explored her womanhood and the wide world.

Never once had she considered accepting a date from another man since Arlon Grey disappeared. There was no room in her heart for another love. She was one of those rare birds that mate for life. She admitted one thing to herself, much to her chagrin. Tara was right; Arlon was still with them both. She felt it way down deep where no one could touch it, a place she visited often in her dreams and quiet moments. A place where true happiness and contentment existed. A place where she could be with the only man she had ever loved.

"What now, Mum? Worked out the letters yet?"

"Not even close. I've sent away samples of the blood to compare it to the other sample I sent."

"Why wouldn't they be the same?"

"Not sure why you think they would be," said Clarice with a frown.

"I just...oh, they can't be, can they? Different writing altogether. At first, I thought our names on the wall was..."

"Was what?" Clarice asked, when it seemed Tara wasn't about to finish.

"A sign," admitted Tara with a sigh.

"A sign...from your father?" Clarice guessed.

"Hmm, yeah," said Tara, sipping her tea. "The opposite is true, though, isn't it? His writing is telling us to go away and whatever that is that you can't decipher. He doesn't want us here," she said glumly.

"You're jumping to a lot of conclusions , young lady, without a shred of evidence to back it up."

"Why write our names on the wall just to tell us to go away, then?"

"Didn't we just establish that the two items are entirely different? You can't chop and change to suit your mood. If, a big if, we are to take for granted that the message for us to go away was written by Arlon somehow, then the other message, our names, was by somebody or something else."

"Wanting to draw us here?"

"Exactly!"

"Who?"

"Well, that's the big question, isn't it? And now a woman has been taken in broad daylight right in front of us: a woman about my height and weight."

"Wait. What does that have to do with anything?"

"Think about it. Two names were written on a wall, and we assume it was to get our attention and draw us here. For what purpose?"

"I assumed it was Daddy and he was wanting to get back to us."

"But?"

"Well, we have to conclude that it wasn't Daddy who wrote our names on the wall. It was... Daddy was trying to warn us, wasn't he?"

"Hard to say."

"Someone wants us…and took a woman about your size."

"Yes."

"You can't blame yourself for what happened," cried Tara in alarm.

"I don't. Doesn't stop me from feeling guilty, though."

"What do you think happened to her?"

"Nothing good."

"You believe we're the targets?"

"Just me, possibly."

"How do you figure that out?"

"My name appearing on a wall by itself may not have lured me here. Your name, appearing in full, might have been just the correct bait. At least for you. I would have had to follow in the event you succeeded in scampering off in the middle of the night."

"Maybe we should go."

"And leave that poor girl out there alone with..." Clarice couldn't bring herself to finish.

"ME?" yelled Graham, as he staggered into the kitchen, reeking of alcohol.

"You, in your current state, yes," answered Clarice fearlessly. "I would be very careful what you say next, Mr Bellows," she said, as he was about to protest. "It could make the difference between retaining custody of your daughter or handing her over to the Child Protection Agency. At present, you are clearly unfit to care for that child, and I would have no qualms about informing the authorities on that score. If, however, you cease becoming inebriated every time something happens beyond your control, and make the effort to be somewhat more courageous for the sake of that little girl, who will need all the help she can get, then I might reconsider."

"I...(burp)..."

"You need to go and have a shower and get cleaned up, shave and all. Then you need about twenty cups of coffee to sober up and something to eat. Once that has been accomplished, we'll talk. Now, do I call the authorities about a neglected child?"

An ear-splitting crack in the air above them shocked them into immobility. A brief shimmering halo, like the ocean's surface on a bright summer's day, hovered over them. Seconds before it disappeared, something bloody and horrible came crashing down upon the table at which Clarice and Tara were seated.

CHAPTER NINE

Neighbours gawked; kids were out in force with a plethora of mobile phones, ready to capture any piece of juicy footage to plaster all over social media. Police had cordoned off the Bellows' residence with blue and white checked plastic tape. The bubble-top flashers of numerous emergency vehicles strobed annoyingly throughout the long day and into the evening.

Clarice, Tara and Graham Bellows had been interviewed several times by different officers attending the scene. Senior Constable Hart and his younger female partner had reluctantly attended, highly suspicious of the weird group who called it in. Jurisdiction of the case was gladly handed over to two homicide detectives from Gladstone.

Cynthia continued to sleep as though dead in the caravan, blissfully unaware of the happenings and the fate of her mother. Tara had been despatched to watch over her. Detectives Hoch and Mercer, two peas out of the same pod, in identical cheap suits, faced Clarice. Hoch had the grizzled look of a man who had attended one too many crime scenes in his career. His slightly younger partner, who had been with him from the beginning of his time in the force, stood quietly to one side with his well-worn notebook in hand.

Clarice wished they would either take them to the local station for questioning or allow them to get off the front lawn, where they were the objects of curiosity and targets for mobile phones. She sighed inwardly at the barrage of questions they had been subjected to and the myriad more to come. She wasn't able to give them the answers they were looking for. There was no way to explain things in a conventional manner that would fit more with their sensibilities and beliefs.

She was growing more impatient by the minute. Her nerves were frayed and she was desperately tired. The day had turned to night, the cadaver recovered from the shambles of a kitchen, the ruined table taken away in pieces as evidence. A phalanx of forensic personnel in navy blue jumpsuits had descended on the scene and continued to search the grounds and interior of the house, bagging anything of interest they came across. Clarice's plaster cast of the foot had been confiscated, along with all her recording equipment. No one believed a word they said.

"Can we go over it one more time, please?" asked Hoch in a smoker's gravelly voice.

"Not sure how many ways we can explain it to you, Detective Hock," said Clarice in a bored tone.

"That's Hoch," he said, emphasising the glottal sound.

"Easy for you to say," observed Clarice drily.

"Well?"

"She fell out of the ceiling, onto the table where we were sitting. I can't get any plainer or clearer than that."

"Ms Grey, you do realise how impossible that sounds to us mere folk who don't believe in goblins, fairies and ghosts? There was no hole in the ceiling, no evidence of anyone having been in the space above, between the ceiling and the roof. We did, however, find a lot of previous damage to the kitchen and many bent implements in the drawers that may have contributed to the condition of the subject."

"Oh? You found an instrument capable of inflicting that particular wound, did you? I find that highly unlikely, detective." She spat out the last word.

"Didn't need to be a single instrument."

"Well, you have a better imagination than I do, then. I had a close look at that wound, and to my way of thinking it was produced cleanly, using only one instrument. Only, I do not know anything as sophisticated and specialised as that. For something to produce a cone..."

"Yes, you've thought of something?" prompted Hoch, as Clarice stopped mid-sentence.

"I was remembering the lump of flesh that we found in the

bathroom the day after we got here."

"What about it?"

"The shape. It could conceivably have come from a wound like the one in Julie Bellows. It was a conically-shaped lump of meat. I took a sample of it and sent it to the lab for analysis. Bimbo and Dumbo over there dismissed it out of hand, saying it was most likely animal flesh."

Hoch smiled at the derogative mention of the two local cops, whom he would be having words with in due course. Their reluctance to investigate the matter professionally, or notify homicide of a possible crime, did not sit well with the older detective. He would be talking to their superior very shortly. Meanwhile, he searched his younger partner's eyes for a hint of sanity in the madness about them. Mercer just shrugged apologetically.

"Are you saying that a lump of human flesh turned up here that could have come from that wound we just saw?" he asked Clarice with a rising inflection.

"No, I didn't say it could have come from Julie Bellows. I suggested it came from a similar wound...or could have. It was two days ago now, way before Julie Bellows disappeared into the wall, then fell from the ceiling."

"Disappeared into a wall and fell from the... You people..."

"I don't care what you make of this, detective, it's the truth, and I won't be changing my story any time soon. You got the same from all three witnesses, didn't you?"

"All three witnesses who could have colluded to come up with a unified alibi."

"Alibi? What would my daughter and I need with an alibi?"

"You tell me. Turns out his wife was leaving him and taking their kid. She'd been planning it for some time, according to her uncle, a Mr Ben Faraday from Melbourne. You have anything to do with that decision?"

"Me?"

"Yeah, how long have you known Graham Bellows?"

"Less than a week."

"So you say."

"Go ahead and check my phone records."

"Already have. Turns out your number has been called from his home phone over a dozen times in the past few months."

"Did you also check the length of those phone calls? Were they even answered? I am not having an affair with Graham Bellows. I heard from him for the first time less than a week ago to engage our services."

"It wouldn't, technically, be 'having an affair', from your end, would it?"

"What's that supposed to mean?"

"You don't have a husband anymore, do you? He seems to have vanished in rather unusual circumstances, according to the rather large file we have on you. Seems you have a lot of trouble following you, including a string of deaths from around eight years ago, at a place called Allies Creek?" ventured the detective with an arrogant air.

"I don't see what any of that has to do with what's happening here, Hock, or Hosh or whatever you call yourself."

"I don't *call* myself anything. It's the name I was born with."

"Super sensitive, huh? I can't pronounce your name. Get over it."

"Why the sudden attitude, Ms Grey?"

"You've just accused me of having an affair with a man I greatly dislike on a personal level. Accused of an implication in the gruesome murder of his wife stemming from that fictitious affair. I was then labelled as something bordering on a serial killer due to unfortunate circumstances surrounding an earlier case I was involved with. Which part of that would you like me to ignore and keep civil about, exactly?"

"I could ask you to accompany me to the station where we can continue this interview."

"Something I have requested repeatedly over the last three hours, Detective Hooch, as an ounce of professional courtesy to get us away from the gawking spectators lapping up every word, soon to be unleashed on all the social media outlets, no doubt."

Mercer shuffled uneasily in the background, sensing the confrontation might become unnecessarily heated in the following moments. Hoch spied the movement in his peripheral vision and recognised the unvoiced signal immediately. The two men knew each other well, and their instincts were honed to perfection over the long period of their partnership.

Hoch breathed in a deep, calming breath. "Buttons?"

Clarice shook her head in consternation. "Huh?"

"The missing buttons on the victim's dress. We assume they were present before she...disappeared into the wall. A floral dress with plastic buttons down the front. Is that correct?"

"How the heck would I know what happened to the buttons, for goodness sake?"

"You agree she wore a dress that buttoned down the front?"

"I guess."

"So, the missing buttons. Any clue as to why they would be missing?"

"You're the detective."

"So are you, according to your licence. Care to use those powers of observation to humour my request?"

"You won't like my answer."

"Try me."

"Inorganic."

"Come again?"

"The buttons, if they were plastic, are inorganic. The dress was 100% cotton, I'm guessing, and that's why it made it through. Notice the teeth?"

"Teeth?"

"Yes, teeth. Those odd little things people have in their mouths. Useful for chewing up food before digestion."

"You can drop the sarcasm any time you like. What about the teeth?"

"No fillings. All dental work, inorganic caps or fillings...gone. The vinyl shoes she wore...gone. Even the alloy jewellery was missing."

"And you're going to shed some light on that sometime soon?"

"Nothing inorganic can pass through the portal."

Hoch was the one to shake his head. He looked at his partner for confirmation that he was hearing correctly. Mercer shrugged again.

"You want to run that by me again in English, please?"

"You said you had a thick dossier on me and my activities. Did they include Arlon Grey's report from our time on Cid Island?"

"Mostly redacted."

"Huh?"

"Above my pay grade, I suppose. A lot of it was classified."

"We were all grilled for weeks after that by some very top brass. We were also made to sign a whole lot of forms, effectively telling us to keep our mouths shut. Something I intend to do about the events on the island, as you do not have the authority to know. If you want me to explain what I think is happening here it will have to be on the understanding that I can't divulge the source of my deductions."

"That sounds a lot like withholding to me..."

"Don't start threatening me, bucko. I've dealt with bigger, meaner, uglier men than you and survived," stated Clarice with hands on hips.

As large as the detective was, towering over the diminutive woman, he stepped back a pace.

"Ma'am? Perhaps you could just give us your insights under the present circumstances without going into those records?" offered Mercer, stepping forward to diffuse the situation.

Clarice recognised the old good cop, bad cop routine for what it was. She wasn't buying it for a second.

"No point. You two just don't have the smarts to accept it. You know there's something out of the ordinary happening here, something conventional thinking won't explain, yet you refuse to accept anything else. I don't want to waste my breath and just be told that I'm a weird chick."

"Look, fair enough. We aren't into all the crap you seem to take for granted, but we need to have some sort of an understanding of what you think is going on here. If we promise not to roll our eyes or make any derogatory comments, will you give us something?" begged Mercer.

Clarice stared at him for long moments before sighing. "I'm not sure I can adequately explain it. Arlon was far better at the science of it than I could ever be. He was a well-read man on most subjects. He was perfect for the kind of work we do. Anyway, it seems to me that something happening here is similar to what we experienced in that file you're talking about. Seconds before any of the events occurred here, a very loud crack of thunder can be heard. I'm sure the neighbours will have corroborated that fact?"

When Clarice received a confirming nod from the two detectives, she continued.

"That sound is an indication of an opening being formed between this dimension, this reality, and another: a portal. It is... I mean, Tara and I have experienced that phenomenon before, and recognised it the moment we heard it, even though I tried hard to deny it. Arlon once explained it to me, but I never quite understood it as completely as he seemed to.

"Nothing inorganic can pass through that portal, according to his research, and if anything organic and alive comes through it into our reality, it reacts badly to our dimension. Sort of like opposite poles coming into contact with one another. I've seen the results of it first-hand. I know you won't believe me, but that's it," said Clarice with a shrug.

"Let's say that we accept what you say for the moment. Why is it happening? What's causing it?"

"There, you have me. I don't know. My daughter firmly believes it is her father attempting to return to us from that other dimension. This house is where my husband spent part of his childhood."

"Why would your daughter think your husband disappeared into another dimension?" said Hoch with disdain.

"Well, when someone you love more than anything on earth is there one moment and vanishes into a shimmering blue haze the next, it kind of makes you believe in the unbelievable. Tara always intuited that her father would someday find a way back to her, to us. This is what she thinks is happening here, only..."

"Only?"

"Arlon Grey is not a monster or a murderer. I don't believe for one moment that it's my husband doing these horrible things."

"That's one hell of a theory," ventured Hoch.

"Got anything better? Is the idea of another dimension that far-fetched to you?"

"Frankly, yes, Ms Grey. Yes, it is."

"Yet almost half of the human population, including you, by the look of that ridiculous thing around your neck, believe in other dimensions already without acknowledging the fact."

Hoch fingered the crucifix showing against his neck, where he had loosened his tie and undone the two top buttons of his business shirt, stained with some kind of condiment.

"I don't know what you're talking about," he said defensively.

"Heaven and hell, detective. You believe in those concepts because you were raised as either a Lutheran or a Roman Catholic, being of German descent. What *are* those concepts you're indoctrinated with but possibly other dimensions? They're certainly not of this realm, are they? You find it okay to believe in a man walking on water, feeding the masses from five loaves of bread and two fish, and finally rising from the dead, but baulk at the mention of a reality other than ours? I find your beliefs more laughable and preposterous than my own...Hooch!"

"Hoch! Detective Sergeant Bradley Hoch, not Hooch," said Hoch, who had run out of patience.

"Steady on, partner. I'm sure the lady doesn't mean to insult you."

"Jeez, stop the act, you two. When will my client be allowed back into his house?"

"When we say so," interjected Hoch. "He can book into a motel for a couple of days."

"He doesn't have the money to book into a motel and he has no friends or family who will take him in. Look at him, he's a mess," said Clarice, pointing to Graham Bellows sitting on the grass holding his head in his hands.

"Not our problem."

"No, the safety and well-being of the public is never your problem, is it?"

"Not when they're a prime suspect in a murder investigation, no."

"Arrest him, then."

"When the time is right, we 'll do just that."

"Oh, give me a break. You have nothing to go on; not a shred of evidence to connect him or any of us to the grisly death of his wife. No murder weapon, no real motive, nothing. You have three eye-witnesses questioned by different officers, all attesting to the same thing and corroborating everything I told you. Fine! If you won't let him back in his own house, and you haven't taken over my caravan, am I free to erect the annex and put him up in there?"

"Getting late, boss. What say we cut them loose for the night and come back tomorrow afternoon?" asked Mercer.

"This afternoon, you mean?"

"Oh, yeah, right," said Mercer, checking his watch.

CHAPTER TEN

Clarice was exhausted by 10 am. Erecting the annex for the first time had tried her patience sorely. Finding enough bedding wasn't a problem, as Arlon had equipped the van with many extras, including a foldaway camp cot which she could set up in the annex for Graham Bellows. Cynthia shared a bunk with Tara while Clarice settled for a well-earned coffee and breakfast as the others dozed.

She wolfed down the hastily-prepared bacon and eggs while sipping her coffee with a look of consternation as she peered at the frozen lump of flesh in the plastic freezer bag. When the police had inappropriately dismissed the find in the bathroom as nothing more than animal meat, Clarice had spirited it away after sending off a sample. It did not diminish her appetite as it should have.

The odd, conical shape, more pronounced in its frozen state, intrigued her. She was unable to imagine the type of implement capable of producing that shape. When Julie Bellows had fallen from or through the ceiling, with her dress flowing open to reveal the cavity in her chest through the top of her left breast, Clarice recognised the shape of the depression immediately.

It didn't look as though anything had been plunged into the victim, more as though something had scooped the flesh out. What had been used, she had no idea.

Clarice had the wherewithal to take a few samples from the cadaver before the police showed up and after the others had exited the kitchen: Graham, to throw up on the lawn out front where he remained during the interrogations; Tara, to keep an eye on Cynthia in the van.

Clarice determined that there had to be another victim somewhere who had lost the cone of flesh on the table in front of her. It could not have come from Julie Bellows, as it had appeared before the woman's disappearance and subsequent murder. That left an uncomfortable lump in Clarice's throat. They were dealing with multiple homicides, possibly a serial killer with some very unusual and gruesome capabilities.

Her mind was in a whirl, trying to make sense of the circumstances and everything they'd witnessed up to that point. Was she right about the aspect of another interdimensional portal? One scrape with the inhabitants of another dimension was surely enough to experience in a lifetime? How plausible was it to suspect she could be facing the same prospect...only worse? Worse, because it appeared as though something more intelligent and malevolent might be at play. So bad that it attracted the warnings from her lost husband?

She had to stop herself thinking along those lines; it only confused her more. Her feelings were preventing her detachment from the case. She found it difficult to concentrate with any degree of objectivity. If Arlon was involved, it could only mean they were in extreme danger. Yes, Clarice admitted to herself, he had gone to that other place. She finally voiced it in her head. She knew Arlon Grey had vanished into the other dimension because of his direct contact with the foreign energy.

She had seen it. She could no longer cling to the premise of denial. Her husband had somehow tapped into that energy, drawing him from their reality. She had to come to terms with that, accept and work with it. Arlon was warning them, albeit with abstract messages, of the dangers to them, to her and possibly Tara, as well. Their names had been written on the wall in human blood to attract their attention, to lure them to Tannum Sands, to the home of Arlon Grey as a boy. What better way to add credence to the lure than by using his childhood home?

Was that the intention of the intelligence behind the attacks? The names were meant to lure them to their deaths, and Arlon Grey somehow figured it out and was warning them to skedaddle? How was any of it possible? Was there another childhood home of another Arlon Grey in the other dimension?

If Clarice went down that line of thought it became too complex, too fraught with never-ending loops of conjecture. It didn't pay to ponder the myriad of possibilities in that scenario. She had no idea what was possible or not in other dimensions. She remembered Arlon saying that, theoretically, there were an infinite number of realities out there, with an equally infinite number of diverse inhabitants. When Clarice dwelled on the memories of the strange creatures they had encountered on that island, she feared the *intelligent* life forms they might have evolved into.

There was sufficient cause to block out most of the horrible experiences from that island, especially the freaky animals. Once she opened that Pandora's box of memories, she shuddered with the possibilities of what else they might yet face. If her husband had survived the last six years in a dimension containing those creatures and what may have evolved from them, it beggared belief. What horrors had he endured and how could he escape? What could Clarice do to help him?

She couldn't voice any of those questions, doubts or theories around Tara. Clarice did not want to hurt the child or build up any hopes in her. They had toughed out the years without Arlon Grey and no one felt the loss more than Tara, though she never displayed it openly. Could Tara have been in some sort of communication with Arlon during that time? She'd admitted as much. Clarice swore she'd felt him at different times, but never heard him, never seen him in anything but dreams? Or were they dreams?

The area outside had quietened considerably in the past hour. She wondered if everyone had gone at long last. She finished the last of her coffee before venturing out of the van, through the annex, making sure to remain very quiet, into the brilliant sunshine. The clouds from the past few days had all dispersed, leaving bright blue skies. Clarice smelled the salt in the light breezes wafting in her direction from the beach.

The gawkers were gone, as well as all the police. The tape had been removed, ostensibly indicating that the house might be available to them. Clarice did not wish to re-enter the house yet; her nerves were still somewhat frayed. Seeing Julie Bellows' lifeless body slamming onto the table directly in front of her would take some time to get out of her immediate memory.

Buttons. She recalled the odd question about the dress buttons and cringed at her explanation even though she believed the answer she'd given was correct. It bothered her that she'd had an answer. It bothered her more that it was probably correct. As much as she hoped it had nothing whatever to do with the forces they had encountered on that island seven years ago, she knew it to be so. Portals to another dimension were opening and closing in their present location and, this time, it wasn't mere animals entering their reality.

There was intelligence at play; their names on the wall were evidence of that fact. The animals they'd once encountered were incapable of that: at least, as far as Clarice could discern. There was also a malevolence about the activities in the small beachside community that they had not witnessed on the island. Julie Bellows had died a gruesome death. It was a deliberate act by the perpetrator, not a defence mechanism, as animals displayed. Julie Bellows had been targeted for some reason, and Clarice felt more and more as though it should have been herself.

Although the Bellows woman was shorter and thinner than Clarice, she suspected that the perpetrator did not know the details of their intended target, did not know what the target looked like. If Clarice and possibly her daughter were the intended victims, it would explain why the girl, Cynthia, had been attacked previously and why Julie Bellows had died. It was conceivable that the murderer mistook them for Clarice and Tara.

It didn't explain why it had been going on for such a long time, nor why the murderer hadn't snatched the females beforehand. If it was as easy as sticking their hands through a portal to grab their victim, as they had Julie Bellows, then why hadn't they done so back at the beginning? Might it be that they couldn't? Had they still been working at the procedure, experimenting, only partially succeeding until recently?

Before Clarice knew it, she found herself walking along the sandy riverbank, soothing waves lapping at the shore. She was near the mouth of the Boyne River, heading east towards the open ocean. On the opposite bank of the river nestled the burgeoning township of Boyne Island, connected by the bridge downstream. Clarice recalled stories her husband had related about the hamlet as it was during his time in Tannum Sands: nothing more than a scattering of homes and one local convenience store.

As Clarice walked along the deserted shore, she noted the many moored vessels dotting the river banks and resting on the lower shoreline, their painters secured to coconut palms festooning the upper dunes. The air was wonderfully warm, calming her for the imminent trials ahead. Clarice sighed heavily, knowing she should leave the area immediately, with Tara, to safeguard her. It was the most sensible thing to do, yet she couldn't make herself accept the logic.

Oddly enough, it was her strong mothering instincts which prevented her from leaving, refusing to leave behind a vulnerable young girl who had just lost her anchor in life. Whether or not the man would break out of his depressed funk to become the father she needed was almost irrelevant. That girl needed her; she needed a woman's support and comfort at this terrible time. The aunt in Gladstone or the uncle in Melbourne might be a solution, or not. It depended on a lot of factors, including the father's agreement.

When Clarice wandered back into the caravan, Tara was up and about, making a brunch for them all, it seemed, by the number of eggs she had placed in the frying pan. Tara was unaware of Clarice's return as she paused to stare at something on the bench. Her mother assumed Tara was simply lost in thought for a moment. When she seemed frozen in place for longer than normal, Clarice touched her shoulder. Tara yelped. Cynthia, who had been watching intently from her seated position, cried out in sympathy.

"Jeez, Mum! Don't sneak up on me like that. You scared ten years out of me."

"I'm so sorry, Tara, and Cynthia. It just...you seemed to be catatonic there for a while."

"Hmm?"

"Well, you were just standing there holding the pan in mid-air. You know those eggs won't cook until you place the pan on the stovetop, right?"

"What? Oh, right," said Tara, placing the pan down.

"When's the crowd coming?"

"What do you mean?"

"There's only the four of us, right? You have more than a dozen eggs in there, Tara."

"Um, hungry," she shrugged.

"I sure hope so. How are you feeling, young lady?"

"Not very good," Cynthia answered shyly.

She was dressed in a simple cotton nightie that belonged to Tara; it ballooned on the diminutive girl. She was clutching a favourite stuffed toy of Tara's, a unicorn, given to her by Arlon after they had attended a local fair. He had won it at a dart booth, where he had collected three balloons with three darts and scored a total of fifty points for his effort. That gave him a choice from the top shelf. Probably costing less than the fee for the game, the unicorn, nonetheless, had become Tara's most prized possession. That she allowed the other girl to hold it spoke volumes of her character.

Clarice watched as Tara expertly whipped the eggs in the pan before placing them on the flame. The toast popped and Cynthia, who had ostensibly been placed in charge, rose to butter the slices. Clarice was pleased that Tara had kept the girl busy.

"Where's our other guest?"

"If you've come from the beach, I'm surprised you didn't cross paths. I sent him for a swim. He stunk to high heaven of sweat and vomit. I bagged up his bedclothes for us to wash later. Cynthia said she would show me how to use her mother's washing machine."

Clarice saw the mention of her mother cause a pang of sadness in the young girl. She wondered how much she knew. She didn't want to broach the subject without finding out what Tara had told her, if anything. The girl's reaction might simply be an ongoing symptom of her mother's disappearance. Clarice would have to consult Graham as well before speaking about anything that had happened the previous night. If he wasn't up to it, she supposed she might have to break the news to Cynthia.

He would have his hands full making arrangements for his wife as well as processing his feelings on top of his daughter's. She knew he wouldn't be up to the task, based on his track record. She hoped she was wrong.

As Clarice glanced back toward Tara, she noticed her frozen stance once more. She was staring intently at the benchtop littered with eggshells, the empty cartons and other kitchen implements.

"What is it, Tara? What's wrong?"

"Nothing, Mum. Why?" asked Tara, emerging from her state.

"You keep freezing in place and I don't think you're even breathing. What are you staring at?"

"You're imagining things. I'm perfectly fine."

"Then would you mind not burning the eggs? I don't like mine well done."

"Oh, shi...shivers," said Tara, quickly stopping herself from swearing in front of her mother.

Tara managed to remove the pan mere seconds before charring the contents. Cynthia smiled at the older girl's near mistake.

"And just what are you smiling at? I thought I put you in charge of brunch, young lady? You nearly let me burn it," said Tara with a huge grin.

The girl giggled. Clarice's heart swelled with pride at the maturity and understanding displayed by her daughter. The three females settled into a congenial banter while they ate their scrambled eggs. Graham Bellows turned up as they were finishing.

"I've left a plate of eggs for you in the oven, Mr Bellows," said

Tara cheerfully.

"I helped make breakfast, Daddy," added Cynthia with a note of hope.

Her hopes were rewarded with a beaming smile from her father. Clarice noted the clean-shaven, nice-smelling person who had returned. His entire demeanour had transformed. The smile for his daughter filled Cynthia with encouragement and a sense of belonging. He was dressed in a tight white T-shirt that showed off a musculature Clarice had not noticed before.

The belly had some signs of a paunch developing, but otherwise, Graham Bellows looked about a hundred times better than previously. Even Tara did a double-take when he entered. The tight jeans he was wearing, the first time Clarice had seen them, indicated to her that he had been inside the house. While that may have set alarm bells ringing for her, it did not seem as though the man had indulged his addictions while he was away.

"Hello, Clarice, and thank you, Tara, I'm famished. How are you, pumpkin?" asked Graham in a kindly tone as he sat down at the table.

"Tara showed me how to scramble eggs, Daddy," answered Cynthia.

"Excellent. I can't thank you both enough for everything you've done for us. The house is going on the market today and I've instructed the realtor to take almost any offer. I... Has anyone said anything?"

"No," said Tara immediately.

"Thanks for that as well. I feel I have to perform that particular task. I can't make the arrangements yet because..."

"Yes, we understand. The medical examiner will have to complete the...procedure before that can be done," said Clarice carefully, to avoid revealing too much in the presence of his daughter. "Tara? If you've finished, I think we should go for a stroll."

"Oh, okay," she answered , recognising the intention.

"Would it be okay if we went into the house to poke around, Graham?"

"No problems. It looks like the police have finished in there. I've booked a cleaning crew to come in later in the day before the realtor gets here. I don't mean to sound rude or ungrateful, but I'm not sure what you hope to gain by continuing to investigate."

"I'm still under contract to come up with some answers, Graham. I intend to honour that contract."

"How can you hope to do that without your equipment?"

"The equipment wasn't recording anything useful, anyway. We've seen more than any of the cameras and heard more than the microphones."

"All the same, I'm releasing you from any further obligations on my part. I'm cashing in what's left of my super and moving out of the house today. I've already found us a little shack near Benaraby until we find something better. A work colleague said we could rent it for a token amount that covers the fundamentals. I've ordered a trailer to pack with our things and borrowed a car to tow it, which I will pick up as soon as I finish this breakfast that our daughters made."

"Wow, you did all that in the short time you were gone having a shower?"

"I had to do some major thinking and planning to prevent any further...hardship to my family," explained Graham carefully.

"I understand that. I'm very pleased to see the real you in action. I'll be continuing with my investigation regardless of your commitment or cooperation, however. I am too invested at this stage to abandon it and I...we," indicating Tara and herself, "have some personal reasons for wanting to remain."

"While I appreciate that, I don't want you to keep going. I don't want my house to end up being unsaleable because of your continuing investigations," Graham warned.

"With all due respect, Graham, did the events begin with our investigations?"

"Well...no," he admitted reluctantly.

"Then what makes you think everything will cease when we're no longer on the case?"

"I...I just..."

"You can't make that assumption. Whatever began in that house will continue until its goal is reached."

"And that is?"

"I haven't determined that yet."

"I'm not leaving without Daddy," said Tara suddenly.

"You can't seriously expect to find your long-lost father out of this? Why are you encouraging this sort of crazy hope in her?"

"One minute spent as a responsible parent and you're giving me advice? I support my daughter and happen to agree with her assessment of the situation. I won't leave here without my husband. You're free to do whatever you wish. All I ask is that you permit me to continue."

"And if I refuse?"

"I'll disobey," stated Clarice with her hands on her hips.

Tara smiled when she saw that familiar stance. It meant her mother would not be swayed. Her ramrod back and fierce expression left no doubt about her resolve.

"Daddy?"

"Yes, love?"

"I don't want to go away. I want to wait here for when Mummy comes back," implored Cynthia.

"You don't understand, Cyn."

"No, she doesn't. You need to talk with her," explained Clarice gently.

"Explain what, Daddy? Has something happened? Did you see Mummy?" she asked with growing concern.

"Now, now, Cyn. I didn't want to upset you any more than you were. It can wait until we leave..."

"I'm not going," she answered, mimicking Clarice's tone of voice.

"You'll go if I say you'll go," warned Graham.

"Isn't it time for you to have another drink, DADDY?" exclaimed Cynthia in her most condescending tone.

"Cynthia! How dare you...?"

"I'm fourteen years old, Daddy. I know you're a drunk. Mummy told me what a coward you are, hiding in a bottle. You may not have had a drink today...yet, but you do want to run away. Well, I won't do it and you can't make me. I won't run away and leave Mummy."

"Fine! You want to see your precious Mummy again, go visit her in the morgue where they're performing an autopsy on her as we speak," shouted Graham with a cruel sneer.

"Mr Bellows! How could you?"

Clarice saw the young girl crumbling at the news delivered in so harsh a manner by her father. She didn't want to believe it, but knew it had to be the truth by the way the others were reacting. Cynthia turned to her new friend, Tara, with beseeching eyes. Tara could do no more than nod sadly, unable to hide the truth.

"You are the worst kind of shit I have ever come across," said Tara to Graham in a whisper, seething with malice.

"That's enough, Tara. I will not have you swearing unless you'd like your mouth washed out with soap."

"Oh, my God, is that even a thing?" Tara asked with revulsion.

"It used to be and can still be a thing if you push me, young lady," warned Clarice without conviction.

"Perhaps if you left for a moment, Mr Bellows?"

"You can't order me about," he snapped.

"In *my* caravan, I can do as I like. I tried being nice, now all I can say is get out before I throw you out. Tara and I will sit with your daughter to help her to understand the situation and what happened. You're not in the right frame of mind to accomplish that task."

Before Graham could say another word or move towards his daughter, Clarice and Tara both moved to come between the pair.

Cynthia had turned ashen and was hyperventilating. While Clarice pushed Graham from the van, Tara administered to the young girl, offering her comfort and soothing words.

"She's my daughter," Graham protested once Clarice and he were outside the van.

"Nice way of showing it," answered Clarice with disdain. "That girl needed her father, her real father, more than anything today. You probably just blew the last chance you had at filling that role. What you just did in there was unconscionable. You tore her heart out and spat on it. It would surprise me if she ever wanted anything to do with you again."

"What, what should I do?" he asked in a pathetic whimper.

"Grow a pair, for a start."

Clarice had to apply mental brakes before she lowered herself to the man's standards. She took a moment as she thought through the mess he'd made.

"Look, your daughter's right about one thing. Running away will not solve this. If whatever force out there thinks your wife and daughter are me and Tara, then they won't stop just because you're heading up the road."

"I don't get why my wife and daughter are targets. It's your names that appear on the walls, not theirs."

"Good, you're thinking again. That helps. Maybe it's playing safe by grabbing any female in the household. Maybe it hadn't quite figured how to accomplish the task until yesterday? I don't have the answers yet, Mr Bellows. I won't stop until I do have them, though."

"I've made a mess of this, haven't I?" he asked, his shoulders drooping, deflating in stature and demeanour.

"Yes, you have. I won't sugarcoat it. That girl in there will probably never forgive you for what you've done to her, over the last six years and, especially, today. I know I wouldn't. If she does come around to accepting you back in her life, she still won't respect you. She will most likely never love and admire you like she does her mother. You'll just have to accept that if you can. If not, you'll have lost it all."

"What do you think I should do? Regardless of what you think, what you've seen, I desperately want to keep hold of my daughter. She's all I have."

"Give her some space for a start. Tara and I will try to mitigate some of the damage you've done. In the meantime, you could save yourself some money by going into that house and straightening it up yourself. I'll help after I've seen to your daughter and made some calls."

"Calls?"

"To get a copy of the autopsy first. Then I have a few other calls to various laboratories regarding the samples I sent out. They may have some preliminary results even though final analysis of DNA won't be available for a time."

"Mum? Do you mind if I go for a drive with Cynthia?"

"How's she doing?"

"About as good as you'd think."

"Where to?"

"Just a drive," said Tara somewhat evasively.

"In Arlon's Prado?"

"No, Mum, your Prado. You pay the rego, the insurance and for all the services. I think it qualifies as yours now."

"I don't know, Tara. You have to have a fully-licensed driver with you on your provisional plates, don't you?"

"If you want to be a total stickler for the letter of the law."

"If you get caught and the car's impounded, you'll be sorry. You'll be walking everywhere for the next ten years."

"Don't be so dramatic. Cynthia just needs some time away from...well, from adults," said Tara, eyeing Graham carefully.

"One hour. Be back by then and you keep your driving privileges."

"No problem, we won't need all of that."

"That implies a destination."

"Don't go all detective on me, Mum. A girl has to have some

secrets from her mother."

"Only if they're the legal kind," warned Clarice, regretting her decision.

She threw Tara the keys with a shake of the head, fearing the worst outcome.

"Can she be trusted with my daughter?" asked Graham sullenly.

"Can you?"

"I..."

"It was a rhetorical question, Mr Bellows."

CHAPTER ELEVEN

Clarice became very concerned as she read the PDF file of the DNA analysis sent to her. She shook her head in consternation, her golden ringlets with greying roots bouncing about in front of her eyes. She swept away the errant bangs to reread the report for the third time. It didn't make any sense and couldn't possibly be true. The oaf of a detective had voiced the connection without knowing what he was talking about.

She and Graham had spent most of the afternoon cleaning the house to a level of acceptable cleanliness, while a repair man mended the broken windows. Graham's haunted eyes had strayed often to relive the scene of horror when his wife had fallen from the ceiling. The kitchen table pieces had all been removed by the forensics crowd. Clarice's foldaway table replaced the timber furniture in the centre of the kitchen.

Clarice sat at the table staring at her laptop in confusion and resentment. She knew the report was not possible; a grave error had occurred. Yet, when she phoned the lab assistant who had performed the test, it was confirmed that the results were accurate. The test had been performed by several members of the team with the same results. The DNA matched, down to the last nucleotide.

Graham hovered by the coffee-maker, waiting impatiently for Clarice to finish reading. She had told him several times to back off, that she would reveal the results as soon as she had finished assessing them. The phone calls she made were infuriatingly uninformative, as he could hear only one side of the conversation. The annoying woman seemed to be deliberately controlling the flow on her side of the conversation to mask whatever truths the report revealed. He knew something important had occurred, for the lady had become quite agitated when she first perused the incoming report.

"Well?" he asked the moment she sat back with a sigh, presumably arriving at a conclusion.

"You won't believe it," she suggested.

"I don't believe any of this, so you may as well spit it out."

"As a complete afterthought, call it a whim, I asked that the two samples I sent be compared."

"What are you talking about?"

"I sent two samples off to the lab for DNA testing. One was from the slab of meat that we found in the bathroom on our first morning here. The other was hair and tissue samples from your wife."

"Tissue samples?" asked Graham, paling.

"A small sliver taken from the site of the wound."

"And?"

"I asked them to do a comparison."

"Why? I don't understand what one has to do with the other."

"They match, Mr Bellows. Not just from the same family or similar. They are identical."

"That isn't possible. They were days apart. My wife was in Gladstone at the time, for heaven's sake! It had to have come from someone else, that first one."

"Not possible. No way two people can have matching DNA. It's an exact science, Mr Bellows. I asked them to rerun the results and have them verified. They were conclusive and unanimous. Both samples were from the same person: your wife."

Graham Bellows' knees gave way slowly. He descended to the kitchen floor with his hands to his head. Clarice was worried he might tip over the edge again. She had found several caches of liquor around the house as they were cleaning up. That wasn't to say she had found them all.

"What can that mean?' he asked breathlessly.

"I can't answer that."

"That seems to be a common reaction from you," he stated with a chilly clarity.

"Dial it back, please, Mr Bellows. You asked me to investigate this matter. I'm doing that. I'm not a bloody magician!" She spoke with an edge of frustration creeping into her voice.

"How did you know?"

"I didn't."

"Then why would you ask the lab to make a comparison?"

"I've already told you. It was a last-minute thing. A hunch, if you prefer. My husband always said it was wise to listen to our hunches because they came from a more instinctual part of the brain."

"Your husband sounds like he was an extraordinary man," said Graham with a hint of derision.

"*Is* an extraordinary man, Mr Bellows, *is*. Anyone having to battle through the condition he was born with and survive would have to have exceptional qualities," Clarice said wistfully.

"I admire your optimism, lady. You still believe your husband is alive and will return to you after six years away. I wonder, though, are you disadvantaging your daughter with that unrealistic faith? I mean, could you be limiting her growth and possible happiness with that?"

"I hardly think that you're qualified to make those kinds of judgments about me, Mr Bellows. I haven't subsided into self-pity and drowned myself in liquid oblivion because of my peccadillos."

"I didn't mean..."

"Oh, yes, you did. You're trying to squirm out of your guilt by offloading some of that on to me. It's wrong to start making comparisons like that. Apples and oranges, Mr Bellows, apples and oranges."

"Okay, you may be right. I apologise. My past behaviour is catching up with me and I have a lot to answer for, not the least of which is my dead wife."

"Not sure you can add that to your list of failures. In fact, had you been a little worse in your behaviour, she might never have returned from Gladstone at your request."

"Not sure how I should take that."

"Whichever way you like. Look, I'm not here to offer you any kind of redemption or forgiveness. I don't know you and I am not your friend. My obligations begin and end with the scope of the investigation and my moral obligation to care for someone unable to do so themselves: your daughter. You may face your demons your way in your time. Whether you face up to the responsibility of caring for your daughter, or not, is up to you when this is all said and done. She needs you even though she rejects and despises you at present."

"She, she despises me?" asked Graham in a shocked whisper.

"Of course. You'll have to work extremely hard to regain even a modicum of respect and trust from that girl. I can't predict if you'll succeed or not. Depends on how you begin to act from here on. A father needs to be a dependable hero for his little girl."

"How do you recommend I go about that?"

"Not my department. I have my pair to care for."

"Pair?"

"Yes, I have another adopted child back home. That boy needs me as much as Tara, if not more. Tara is getting to the stage where she might not need me as a mother as she used to. She has a mind of her own now and can be quite wilful. Part of growing up, I suspect. I went through that stage at approximately the same age. Your daughter is not that far away from it. You need to mend your bridges before she flies the coop."

"Mixing metaphors there."

"Perhaps. Never laid claim to being scholarly."

"How does the report help us?" asked Graham, to change the subject.

"Not sure that it does. How the chunk of flesh turned up days before your wife's unfortunate demise is a complete mystery."

"Shouldn't we inform the detectives about it? Give them the evidence you concealed from them?" he stated with a touch of recrimination.

"You never let up, do you? If your memory serves, you'll recall that I did everything but go down on my knees to beg the police to bag and tag the evidence that morning."

"Not to them local idiots. I was talking about the Gladstone detectives. You didn't admit to keeping the evidence or offer it to them."

"Knowing what we know now, I'm glad. It would only have clouded the issue. Too many odd facts and everyone ends up chasing their tails."

"Doesn't look to me like you're doing anything different."

"All right! Have it your way," said Clarice, rising from her chair.

"What?" asked Graham, startled by the sudden movement.

"You get your wish. I'm packing up and leaving the moment Tara returns. Which reminds me, she's been gone a long time."

"Why?"

"You can't seriously be asking me that? You've been telling me to leave almost since I got here. You've not shown me the slightest bit of courtesy or respect. The scorn and derision have not gone unnoticed, Mr Bellows. I thought I could weather it, but it turns out I'm human after all. I don't need this bulldust in my life. As I just informed you, I have another little person waiting for his mummy to return to him. Time I acted responsibly to do just that."

Clarice stormed out of the house, to be greeted by two beaming girls exiting the Prado, each with fully-laden arms carrying things Clarice couldn't immediately identify.

"Where have you been?"

"Well, hello to you too, Mum," answered Tara, not about to be dragged down by her mother's foul mood.

Tara ignored her mother's scowl and continued unloading cartons from the rear of the car on to a small hand cart. She then wheeled the cart to the rear of the property.

Clarice followed the pair. "Pack your things, Tara. We're off."

"No, please, you can't," cried Cynthia.

"Listen, pet. Your father doesn't want us here anymore and I have pressing matters at home. My boy needs his mother and we just aren't appreciated here."

"Please don't go. *I* need you. I need you more than ever. I don't have anyone else who can help me," begged the girl.

"Mum, what happened?" asked Tara, realising her mother was serious.

"Never mind. What is all this?" she asked, indicating the cardboard boxes Tara had stacked in front of the annex, next to some carpet rolls.

"I figured some of it out," answered Tara cryptically.

"Figured what out?"

"The message, Mum. I figured out the first bit of the message. The one with the smudged letters?" Tara prompted when she saw the look of confusion.

"Oh. And?"

"Egg cartons. You were right about 'egg' being the first word. Egg cartons. Don't you see?"

"Sure, all makes so much sense now. Egg cartons, of course! How silly of me."

"I didn't say I knew everything," admitted Tara glumly.

"What does egg cartons have to do with anything, Tara? What has gotten into you? And the carpet?"

"I...don't know...yet."

"You sound like a fruit cake."

"Does a fruit cake make a sound?" asked Tara.

"Don't try to be funny with me, young lady. We have to leave. Our services here are no longer required or appreciated."

"They are required, by her," stated Tara, with a finger pointing at Cynthia. "And since when does it matter if you're appreciated? That sounds more like a blow to the ego than anything professional. Daddy would never bother with someone's opinion about either him or his abilities. He would just do the job he was asked to do. Didn't he always warn us about letting our emotions rule us?"

"That's not fair, Tara. He wasn't weighed down by emotions.

He didn't have any."

"What's fair? Is it fair that any of this happened to Cynthia and her family? Is it fair that we may be the cause of it? Is anything in life fair? I think it was you who said that. Well, it's only good advice if you practise what you preach."

"Tara!"

"Hey, you're the one who keeps teaching me to think for myself and stand up for what's right. This isn't like you, Mum. You don't run from a fight. You and Daddy both hammered that one into me. The only one who loses..."

"Is the one who runs away, only to get beaten up another day," said Clarice, finishing the silly saying Arlon came up with. "It's not a wise saying, Tara. Sometimes it's best to retreat," she said half-heartedly.

"Please stay," begged Graham, as he came up to the group in the rear yard. "I'm sorry I've been a pain in the butt. Cyn? What I said to you was unforgivable, I know. So I won't ask you to forgive me. I'm so, so sorry for what happened and that I couldn't do anything to prevent it. I'll try very hard from now on to be the sort of father you can at least depend on. You're all I have now. I know you have your aunt in Gladstone and your great uncle in Melbourne, and, if you prefer to stay with one of them, I'll understand. I hope you'll give me a chance, though."

Although Cynthia's tears were flowing freely, she managed a smile for her father. Clarice thought there might be a chance for the two of them as long as Graham kept to his word and stayed off the grog.

"I, I want to help them, Daddy," said Cynthia quietly.

"What is it you have there?"

"My daughter says she worked out part of the message. Remember I said the first three-letter word could be either erg, eng or egg?"

"I thought you said you weren't positive it was a three-letter word?"

"I wasn't. Tara says the first two words are 'egg cartons', which has me as mystified as you appear to be. I was waiting for an explanation before you came out. Well?" asked Clarice, waiting for Tara to elucidate.

"All I can tell you is that I had to go and get egg cartons and carpet. I don't know why yet," she admitted reluctantly.

"You..."

"Hold on, Mr Bellows, let me get to the bottom of this. Tara, you do know how strange that sounds, right?"

"Yep...yes," she corrected herself when she saw the look on her mother's face.

"Well?"

"It came to me last night."

"This is like pulling teeth," stated Clarice, when no more information was forthcoming. "Tara, please stop drawing this out and tell me everything, no matter how it sounds or what anyone might think."

"I couldn't remember the dream I had when I woke this morning. It was only when I started making breakfast that parts of it slowly came back to me."

"I *thought* you were acting a little out of character when I came into the van. I caught you staring at something a couple of times, as though you were in a trance or something."

"Yeah, I was remembering some of it...sort of. It was more of a feeling than pictures, though. As if I was being pushed to get egg cartons and then, later, carpet."

"Tara, spit it out."

"It was Daddy, okay? I swear it was Daddy pushing me to get those things, only I don't remember clearly."

"Tara..." Clarice shook her head in frustration, trying her hardest not to show the disappointment she felt. "Is that where you went?" she asked eventually.

"There's a poultry farm just out of town off the main road. I spent the money you gave me for wages on them."

"How did you even know about it?"

"Googled it," she said with a shrug.

"And the carpet?"

"Offcuts from a carpet layer in town. Googled that as well. It wasn't hard. Sorry we took so long."

"Let's say I accept what you say for the time being. What's the plan? What are we going to do with all those egg cartons and carpet?"

"That's the part I don't know yet. He'll tell me."

"Has someone just left the reservation here, or am I missing something?" asked Graham.

"As kooky as it sounds, Mr Bellows, I have to ask you to give my daughter some leeway. She has a special connection with her father that's impossible for me to adequately explain or deny. A lingering sensation comes upon me at times, but it's not as strong or as detailed as what Tara is experiencing. That writing on the wall is in my husband's hand; there's no getting around that. It wouldn't surprise me at all to know that he is helping us somehow from wherever he is."

"Daddy?"

"Yes, Cyn?"

"I trust Tara and Mrs Grey. I..."

"What is it, Cyn?"

"Tara helped me."

"Helped you how?"

"I couldn't stop crying when you told me about Mummy. I was really upset and couldn't breathe properly. Tara put her hand on me and I felt heat...and then I started to feel better. And..."

"And?"

"I felt..." she stammered shyly.

"Felt what, sweetie?"

"Him...her father. I felt what she was feeling and I knew it was going to be all right. He's trying to help us, Daddy."

"Tara? How...?"

"I think some of it transferred to me through Daddy," admitted Tara with a shrug.

"This is going back into kooky land. Not sure how much of this I can take," muttered Graham.

"Mr Bellows..."

"Graham, for goodness sake. Graham!"

"Okay. Graham, I know how this must sound to you but I trust my daughter implicitly to be telling the truth. Something affected us all on that island, and it caused my husband to vanish into thin air. My daughter and I experienced a little of that same...energy: maybe Tara more than me. Tara and Arlon were very close: as close as it's possible to get for two unrelated people."

"You're saying my daughter is affected by that now? That she's going to vanish?" said Graham with more than a hint of desperation.

"No, that's not what I'm saying at all. Arlon managed to heal someone with serious injuries using that force, leaving no residual evidence of its use. I can't explain how it happens or why, I can only say that the energy is relatively benign...so far."

"So far?" said Graham, picking up on the uncertainty.

"No studies are being conducted on us or the recipients of the energy, so there's no way to tell with absolute conviction that there won't ever be any repercussions. The authorities never believed our stories, even though they made us sign all sorts of NDAs and national security forms. Surely, if it made your daughter feel better, it can't be all that bad?"

"Without a parent's permission, I would say performing any kind of...alteration was unconscionable."

"Seeing as 'the parent' was the cause of the problem, I'm sure Tara felt justified in doing what she could to assist a distraught young girl," said Clarice, an edge creeping into her voice.

"I'm fine, Daddy. Please don't be upset with Tara or her mother. At least they're trying to help," said Cynthia with a little more confidence.

"Meaning I'm not trying to help?"

"More like the opposite," she admitted.

Graham sighed. "My little girl *is* growing up. I guess, I'd better do some growing up too, huh?" he said with a wan smile. "I'm glad you feel a bit better, but don't forget your mum altogether. She loved you very, very much."

"I couldn't ever forget Mummy," she said sadly.

"It just looks as though you seem to be coping too well, that's all."

"Are we in a contest to see who feels the worst now?" asked Clarice impatiently. "You get the gold badge, okay, Graham. You feel the worst. Happy now?"

"That's not what..."

"Skip it. Just try to remain positive and remember that, however mature your daughter seems, she is still only fourteen. Whatever Tara did to assuage her grief earlier won't last forever, and she'll need a strong, mature, loving father to assist her through the rest of it."

"Got it. I'll do my best. Now what?" he asked, straightening his posture.

CHAPTER TWELVE

Glunk, glunk, glunk.

The onerous sound penetrated their senses on every level. It thrummed through the ears and the pores, spearing into the flesh and bones beneath the epidermis. Cynthia cried out in alarm, clutching Tara with all her might.

Clarice knew it had been a mistake to allow the girl to accompany them into the house, into the kitchen again, waiting for the enemy to strike. Graham's eyes were saucers, while Tara remained calmest of all. They had just finished eating dinner. The light was quickly fading outside. Storm clouds gathered once more, obscuring the moon.

The ear-shattering crack above their heads shocked the small party to the core. The small pool of shimmering blue appearing just under the ceiling captured their rapt attention. The head that came through that pool was like nothing on earth. It was truly the monster that Cynthia had described, with elephantine-grey skin in flaps covering a face devoid of eyes or hair. The most outstanding feature was its grotesque mouth full of canines extending forward, mincing in a circular motion beyond any human capabilities.

The group crashed out of their chairs and backed up quickly against the walls. Suddenly remembering the way Julie Bellows had been grabbed from behind through one of those walls, they moved away a pace or two. Cynthia had ceased her cries, frightened into silence, and was clutching Tara for dear life.

The monster poking its ghastly head through the portal did not appear to be 'seeing' them. Instead, its throat bobbed up and down to produce the sounds they all heard and feared: a deep glottal strumming. The head turned in Cynthia's direction, causing the girl to scream once more. Tara moved to stand in front of her.

A hand shot through the opening, flexing, grasping, reaching for the two girls.

Glunk, glunk, glunk.

The sound pierced their eardrums as it reverberated through them like a tangible entity. The electric lights flickered and a bluish light filled the kitchen from the mirage-like gateway. Clarice recognised the event as being similar to the experiences they had encountered on the island: the same preceding crack of thunder as the portals appeared, the same effects. Only a different creature was trying to come through.

That it had an intelligence was not in doubt. That it was sentient had yet to be determined. The electricity in the house behaved sporadically, turning on and off to match the pulses from the pool of mesmerising light. The microwaved pinged, the blender blended, and the kitchen drawers slipped in and out.

Clarice kept her head, observing that the creature did not seem to want, or be able, to extend fully through the portal to reach them. If it knew what had happened to other creatures that exited the other dimension, then it was right to fear the consequences. However, Clarice felt she might be affording the creature more intelligence than it deserved. The long, skinny hand, tipped by needle-point nails, reached toward the pair of girls huddled together as far away as possible, against the kitchen cupboards.

Glunk, glunk, glunk.

The sound was making them nauseous. It plunged into their innards like a physical blow, vibrating their bones. It was the worst feeling Clarice had ever experienced. It made her want to curl into a foetal ball. The expressions on the other faces mirrored her own as the agony became almost too much to bear. Their knees were buckling as they succumbed to the debilitating waves of sound.

Unable to reach its objective, the creature moved forward, extending its body further into the kitchen, advancing nearer to the girls.

That was Clarice's cue to move. She could see her daughter being threatened. Her motherly instinct kicked into overdrive to overcome the forces disabling her. She reached deep into her reserves and launched herself across the kitchen to the cutlery drawers by the sink.

Disregarding the top drawer, holding general cutlery, she opted for the lower drawer, which contained butcher's knives. She seized on the first one she came across, a cleaver. Swiftly hoisting it from the drawer, she swung it round in an arc to strike the arm that was now so close to the girls cowering before it.

The blow glanced off the creature's arm with no discernible impact. The only clue that it had felt anything at all was the arm's slight change in direction, aiming towards Clarice. The hand raised its ugly, elongated digits with the lethal points towards the new target. She felt the waves of new sound being directed solely at her. They threatened to immobilise her and cause untold damage internally.

Desperately, the world about her darkening as she began to fade into unconsciousness, Clarice raised the cleaver once more. Using every ounce of her waning strength, she aimed it at the gap between the digits on the hand. Instinct drove the cleaver into the softer, fleshier purlicue between the thumb and index finger, if those terms could be applied to the creature. The tip of the cleaver sliced deeply through the area.

All sounds stopped immediately and the head reared back into the pool of light. The hand shook, the wound bleeding profusely. The glimmering pool snapped shut without fanfare, leaving the thrashing limb behind, severed cleanly from the body at a point close to the shoulder. An instant later, the arm imploded in a spray of blood and tissue, coating the foursome in gore.

The group was stunned, grimacing with revulsion. Graham had paled considerably, shaking with fear. Tara and Cynthia remained huddled together on the floor against the kitchen cupboards. Clarice, still holding the meat cleaver in a white-knuckled grip, stood frozen with shock.

Recalling the ugliness of the creatures she had witnessed back on the island, she didn't think it was possible to see anything worse. She was wrong, very wrong.

Another crack sounded outside the house. The group jolted as though hit by an electric shock. Movement at the kitchen door leading to the back yard alerted them that something was trying to enter the house. Clarice moved first, grabbing one of the kitchen chairs to wedge under the doorknob. She turned the key in the centre of the knob to engage the deadlocking device.

Something thumped solidly against the outside of the door. They gasped in unison. Sounds at various points around the outside walls indicated more than one presence. A sudden pounding overhead caught their attention.

"There's one of them on the roof," Graham almost squealed.

"I'm aware of that, Graham. However, panicking will not solve anything. I need you to calm down. I've proven that they aren't invulnerable. They can be hurt."

"I think you got lucky, Mum. Did you see the way it just bounced off its skin the first time?"

"Yes, I did. I also saw the cleaver chopping through that softer bit of its hand."

"You didn't chop its arm off," accused Graham.

"I didn't say I did. I only wounded it slightly. The closing portal took the arm and the interdimensional disparity took care of the rest," stated Clarice with confidence.

"What the hell does that mean?"

"Not now, okay? I'll try to explain later...if there is a later."

"Mum?"

"I don't think they liked what happened one little bit. I think they sent reinforcements. More than one out there," said Clarice, as they all strained to make out the different areas of sound and movement.

A thump outside one of the windows alerted them to the possibility that the one on the roof had just jumped off. The sound of tapping on the glass of the window in the lounge room confirmed their suspicions. That was the window where Clarice had found the footprint...only, she'd found that footprint days ago.

Clarice felt her head spinning with that piece of illogical information. She sprinted from the kitchen to the lounge room and peered through the window. She glimpsed a very tall figure vanishing into another blue halo of light, which winked out of existence the moment it was through. Clarice paled. Unless her eyesight was playing tricks on her, the creature would have been nearly three metres tall, ten feet or more on the old scale.

The others had followed Clarice into the lounge room.

"Mum? What is it?" asked Tara when she saw the fear on her mother's face.

"It...they...are enormous. Way taller than humans. And..."

"And?"

"Something weird is happening here."

"That's the understatement of the century," remarked Tara.

"No, even more than the obvious stuff. Backwards."

"What do you mean?"

"It...it's happening in reverse...or something."

"I have no idea what you're talking about."

"That makes two of us," added Graham.

"Three," from Cynthia, holding up four fingers, which made them all smile.

"I don't want to discuss this in front of the children," stated Clarice.

"You think we could be any more spooked than we are?" asked Tara incredulously.

Clarice looked at each of the faces, all concentrating on her, and received nods of agreement with Tara's announcement.

"You kids don't know this. The chunk of...flesh we discovered the morning after our arrival? It came from...Julie Bellows."

"Mum, no, that can't be right. Mrs Bellows was nowhere near here then," offered Tara.

"That's what I mean. Stuff is happening backwards here. I sent away samples of that flesh and other samples of Julie's hair and skin after she...you know? They are an exact DNA match."

Cynthia attempted to hold back a sob, unsuccessfully until Tara placed a hand on her cheek. The girl immediately relaxed. Clarice wasn't sure she appreciated or agreed with whatever Tara had done. Arlon's use of that...energy or healing ability had caused him to vanish. She was extremely fearful that the same thing would happen to her daughter.

To avoid thinking about what she had just witnessed, Clarice continued.

"I'm betting that thump we heard when that thing jumped off the roof is what caused those prints we discovered under the window. There weren't any tracks leading away from the site because that thing exited straight into one of those portals. I'll bet you anything you like, if we go out to investigate under the window, we'll find only one set of prints. Whereas, by rights, there should now be two sets."

"What does it mean?" asked Graham in a whisper.

"Why are you whispering? I think they're all gone. I can't hear any more movement or sound out there."

"Mum, how can that be possible? It doesn't make any sense. A piece of...you know...shows up before it happens and then footprints show up days before they were made?"

"Yes, it is impossible...in our time."

"Huh?"

"I believe there's a time element involved here."

"You wanna run that by me again?" asked Graham, harbouring a shipload of doubts.

"Explain it another way?" Clarice offered. "Something is cockeyed here. I can't think of any other cause for what we're experiencing."

"Wow! Time travel. Cool," ventured Tara with a grin.

"Or distortion. Not cool at all, considering what we're dealing with."

"Why the distinction?" asked Graham.

"I'm not sure the goal is being achieved. It's causing a temporal malfunction. I think it ties in with the events on the island to a certain degree. Tara and I saw some weird and dangerous creatures appearing from interdimensional portals created by an interstellar, interdimensional asteroid that found its way to earth many millions of years ago."

"I thought you said that was all classified?"

"Too bad. We're facing similar circumstances and I can't see the point in secrecy right now. Besides, who are you going to tell who will believe you?"

"Good point," he admitted with a sigh. "What did you mean earlier about the disparity taking care of the rest?"

"You saw what happened to that hand?"

"Yeah," agreed Graham, wiping a little more gunk from his bare arm with disgust.

"Arlon explained that phenomenon to us as being an interdimensional disparity. When sufficiently exposed, organic matter coming into contact with another dimension reacts explosively. It's like opposites reacting to one another. Those creatures we saw only survived in our dimension for short periods. Often they imploded upon entry. Others suffered the reaction when part of their inner anatomy was exposed to our elements. I suspect these...beings we are seeing are protected to a certain degree by the armoured flesh they have. But you saw what happened to the arm. The portal closing prematurely cut clean through it, armour and all. The disparity of our opposing elements coming into direct contact with the raw flesh caused the reaction we saw. This is possibly why I have never fully accepted that my husband could still be alive. If he did recede into another dimension, somehow, I couldn't see how he could have survived. What goes for them must certainly be universal."

"So you think your husband went the same way as that hand did?" asked Graham.

"In a way, I hope so."

"Mum!"

"It's fast, Tara. Better than prolonged suffering."

"Then who's writing on the walls?" asked Tara pointedly.

"Can we be truly certain it's him, Tara? Can't there be another explanation? The similarity in writing style is close, I'll grant you that. Beyond coincidental as well, given the location. I just..."

"You're wrong, Mum. You know you're wrong and just can't accept it. It's Daddy. I know he's alive, and I know how."

"What? Tara, what are you saying?"

"You know as well as I do that Daddy was imbued with that energy. We both saw it. That energy came from the other dimension, didn't it? That allows him to survive wherever he went. He's a part of it. Not opposite."

"Tara that's...that's... actually, I can't fault that reasoning. Not sure where you got the word 'imbued' from. Last time I checked you weren't doing all that well in English. Your theory holds water, though, if it's true."

"So let me get this straight. Somehow your husband has broken through to another dimension, survived, and turned into Doctor Who, or something?" asked Graham with incredulity etched into his features.

"I didn't say that Arlon had travelled in time. I said that there was a skewed time element involved with the incidents occurring here. That much is pretty indisputable."

"According to your beliefs."

"I don't know how a piece of your wife could show up days before her disappearance without that distortion. Do you?" Clarice shot back.

While it stopped him in his tracks, unable to refute her claims, Graham remained sceptical and obtuse in his manner. He did not like where the conversation was heading. He believed he was made of better stuff than to accept the airy-fairy tales being bandied about with such flagrant disregard for logic, science and common sense.

He was perfectly willing to accept the presence of ghosts or a house retaining some past spiritual energy derived from evil. He had a certain amount of faith and could be pushed to believe in lost souls seeking redemption or revenge. There were many unexplainable phenomena in the world today.

However, he lived in Australia during the twenty-first century, and not some futuristic land where people could teleport in and out of dimensions or through time without the convenience of a Tardis. Those sorts of wild notions belonged in books and on the boob tube, not his home, not his mind, not now, not ever!

Graham had already lost his wife. While the course of events had assisted to delay his devastating grief, he felt the edges of that malaise creeping through. He watched as his daughter was being held by the girl, who was somehow keeping Cynthia calm. The girl almost seemed to glow. If he wasn't mistaken, she had an aura about her: a pale halo of bluish-white light.

Graham knew his daughter had not yet grieved for her mother, either. That girl was preventing it. An instant ire tore through him at that thought, making him rise to the pair huddled together against the kitchen cupboards. Graham yanked his daughter away from Tara's clutches with a look of steely determination.

"Time we left, Cyn. I'll take you to your uncle in Melbourne. He'll care for you while I find a job and a place for us to stay."

Cynthia tore from his grasp. "No, Daddy. It won't help, we'll still be in danger. It's after us."

"No. It's after them! Their names are on the wall, not ours. This crap can't go on. We have to leave," argued Graham impatiently, reaching for his daughter's hand.

She shied from his outstretched hand. "We have to prepare," she stated calmly and mysteriously.

"Prepare? Cyn, this is..."

"Sorry, Daddy. I'm staying here with them. I want you to stay as well."

CHAPTER THIRTEEN

Graham ended up staying. Clarice ended up staying. The girls were being secretive, with strict instructions for neither Clarice nor Graham to ask questions or interfere. They had commandeered the caravan annex, refusing to let anyone enter. The industrious pair were heard making all manner of crafty sounds from within, while the adults stood about scratching their heads.

Clarice had made a slew of phone calls without gaining any new information. She was on her way to interview a neighbour when Graham emerged from the house after another round of cleaning, repairing and replacing. The new realtor sign dominated the front yard, announcing the prime riverfront property with all the accompanying details and phone numbers.

It surprised Clarice how quickly the agents had descended on the new listing to take their pictures, and for all the agency's sales staff to parade through the house to familiarise themselves with the salient selling points: namely location, location, location. If they were aware of the 'hauntings', they never let on, fake smiles plastered on their faces throughout the spectacle. Commercialism at its worst, thought Clarice. Vultures, ready to pounce and take advantage of a family's tragedy.

It seemed to Clarice that Graham had turned a corner. There was no evidence of him falling off the wagon, or coming apart at the slightest difficulty. Granted, his difficulties were onerous, but he was coping for the time being.

As the afternoon waned, no one particularly wished to re-enter the house. Fear gripped Clarice and the others differently; however, it was clear from the drawn faces that all were affected to a large degree. Crossing the lawn to walk to the neighbour's house, Clarice was forced to recite the lady's name a few times to commit it to memory. Mrs Faith and Mr Henry Denham, leaning towards their later years, were pensioners and avid gardeners, according to Graham.

As Clarice entered the Denham yard via the small wrought-iron gate in the white picket fence, she saw evidence of the gardening claim in the pristine beds bordering a manicured lawn. It always amused Clarice when she heard the term 'manicured lawn', thinking it a gross exaggeration, until she spied Mrs Denham at the edge of the lawn with a pair of scissors doing precisely that. A giggle almost escaped her lips, which she clamped shut with difficulty.

"Mrs Denham?" she asked when she had her fit of the giggles under control.

Faith looked up from her labours with a look of surprise, despite being forewarned and fully prepared for a visit from the next-door neighbour's private detective. Faith Denham had all but fallen from her front window several times attempting to take everything in that was occurring next to their house. It was the most excitement the neighbourhood had seen in all the time she'd been there. Although excitement might not be the best word to describe the very sad events of late.

Faith had grown to like Julie Bellows since they moved in and had an adorable baby. Unfortunately, their friendship had never had the chance to truly develop with all the goings-on taking place: police arriving at all hours, rows between the couple, awful sounds without an explanation. Faith had advised an exorcism by her local parish priest on numerous occasions, to no avail. Both Mr and Mrs Denham could not place a foot on the property next door for fear of an evil presence, a demon residing there, possibly even the devil himself. They crossed themselves every time they exited their front gate

Mrs Denham was wearing a floral print dress. Daisies, thought Clarice, as she advanced along the path with a hand outstretched in greeting.

"My name is Clarice Grey, Mrs Denham. I believe Graham may have called ahead to announce me?"

Faith raised the brim of her floppy straw hat to better see the delightful woman, whom she was led to believe could be a private detective.

"Hello. Yes, Graham called me this morning to say you might come over for a chat. Delighted to meet you," she said in a kindly tone, with a beaming smile of false teeth and breath that would knock over a buffalo. "Would you like to come inside for a cup of tea?"

"Oh, I wouldn't want to put you to any trouble, Mrs Denham."

"Call me Faith, please. No need for all that formality. Clarice, was it? No trouble at all and I'm due for a break."

"You have a very beautiful garden, Faith. It must keep you both very busy."

"Labour of love, dear. Henry and I adore being out in the fresh air, pottering around the gardens. We keep a greenhouse in the back for Henry's orchids. I look after the mundane stuff while he gets accolades for his prize blooms at all the shows," Faith stated with a weary sigh.

"Well, yours is by far the more striking contribution if you ask me. Anyone looking into this yard would be very impressed with your hard work and attention to detail. Not to mention your meticulous attention to the lawn," suggested Clarice, nodding toward the pair of scissors in Faith's hand.

"Oh, I know how it must look," she said with a titter. "I just can't abide those electric or petrol edging tools that Henry uses. I find I can't handle them at my age, so a good pair of hardy scissors does the job splendidly, and I don't have to rely on menfolk to maintain my lawn," she said with a satisfied smirk.

The interior of the house overwhelmed the senses. Floral prints on the wallpaper, chintz upholstery on the lounge, more flowers on the curtains, coloured plaster ceiling rosettes, artificial arrangements and vases with real blooms adorned almost every space and surface. To Clarice, it was a nightmare. If forced to live in the Denham house she would be ill the entire time. It was a test of her willpower to remain indoors.

Faith proceeded into the kitchen, indicating the dining table for Clarice as she prepared the tea. The floral theme continued throughout the house, with the rich bouquet of fresh flowers, especially the roses, filling the nostrils. Trying to keep her eyes trained on the table in front of her, Clarice wondered how anyone could cope with the confronting decor.

"I heard about poor Mrs Bellows, and saw the police and ambulance, of course. So sad," remarked Faith as she busied herself in the kitchen.

"Yes, tragic for her daughter and husband. Did you know her well?"

"Got along like a house on fire when she first moved in next door. Darling little daughter came along soon after, then..."

"Then?" Clarice prompted.

"Well, then all that domestic stuff happened. So prevalent nowadays among the young folk. Fighting and arguing, sometimes all night. I just can't understand it. If Henry and I disagree on something, we discuss it, agree to disagree and get on with our lives. Young folks don't have the same respect for one another these days. Such a pity," she said with a sigh.

"Did you have any idea what caused the problems?"

"Oh, I couldn't say, could I?" she asked rhetorically.

"Couldn't as in didn't know?"

"Now, as a close neighbour I couldn't help overhearing certain things, but it wasn't my place to comment or interfere."

"But you did, didn't you? You called the police several times with complaints of domestic disturbances?"

The rattling of crockery from the kitchen indicated that Clarice had struck a nerve.

"I'm quite sure you're mistaken, dear," she stated tartly.

"Oh? I'm not attempting to make accusations. After all, it's a civic duty to bring attention to possible abuse happening in your neighbourhood. I've seen the police reports, Faith."

The elderly woman frowned in consternation and some guilt as she debated telling the truth to the stranger at her dining table. It had been a trying ordeal living next to the Bellows family. There were many occasions where she had been forced to call the police with a complaint, something she was assured would be kept confidential. That the female detective had seen the reports first-hand bothered Faith more than she could say. Though she ached to discover the truth behind the latest calamity to strike her neighbour, she was acutely embarrassed by the woman's revelations.

Taking her time to gather her thoughts as she poured the boiling water from the kettle into the teapot, Faith had no option but to accept that she had been identified as the troublesome neighbour. The sigh that escaped her told of her frustration and embarrassment.

Once the tea had rested for sufficient time, Faith carried the tray of cups and pot over to the table. "I didn't want to become known as one of 'those' types of nosy neighbours who keep meddling in the affairs of the family next door," she admitted sheepishly.

"I understand fully. I'm not here to make a judgement call on that or anything else. I'm only here to gather your thoughts on the events next door leading up to the tragic death of Mrs Julie Bellows. I would very much like to prevent any further tragedies from happening there or anywhere else in the neighbourhood."

"You, you think there is a possibility of that?" asked Faith with a pallid expression.

"I didn't say that and I hope not. Nothing so far suggests that anyone else is in danger," explained Clarice in a calm and kindly tone. She sipped the aromatic tea, nodding and murmuring her acknowledgement of the superb taste. "Excellent tea, Faith. I don't go so much for tea anymore, which is possibly because I went the teabag route."

"Can't abide bags. Has to be fresh tea of a particular selection steeped properly in the pot."

"Have you heard anything other than the arguments coming from next door, Faith? Sounds, movements, that sort of thing? Seen anything out of the ordinary?"

Faith considered the question for a moment, nodding as she did. "I've heard frightful sounds coming from there. Sounds I couldn't place, demonic. Not that I can say I'm an authority on demonic sounds, mind?"

"Go on," prompted Clarice.

"It seemed to start with the young girl having awful night-mares. Her screams woke me often. Our bedroom is close to the girl's. Henry and I thought there may have been...something ...untoward happening at first. So we called the police. Turns out the police had mostly been contacted by the Bellows, in any case. I asked if they could keep my name out of it. I just wanted to protect the young lass, you see? That was my only concern. What the adults do to each other is their affair. It just shouldn't reach the young."

"Tell me, have you heard the loud noises that have nothing to do with arguments?"

"You mean, like the thunder and lightning without a storm?"

"Lightning?"

"Well, not normal lightning, that's for sure. Very bright, bluish light in the middle of the night sometimes, lighting up the whole neighbourhood. Thumping sounds and strange gurgling. Enough to make a body shiver and cross myself. I have never been closer to the Lord than in the last few years. As if that place hasn't seen enough strangeness in its lifetime."

"What do you mean?"

"There was a family in there a long time ago, just after Henry and I moved in. They were a pair, those two. Their son never could do anything right by his parents. He was a queer sort, but gentle and never said a word wrong, always so polite," said Faith as she drifted off into her memory.

"I don't suppose you're talking about the Greys?" ventured Clarice.

"Why, yes. However could you know? I think the son's name was Arnold...or something like that."

"Arlon. Arlon Aloysius Grey."

"That's it. Arlon. Never forget those blue eyes. Stare straight through a body, they would. How on earth would you know that?"

"He was...is my husband. My name is Clarice Grey and my husband spent part of his youth in that house. It's, it's what drew me here in the end."

"Well, I never. How is he? Why isn't he here with you? Oh, I'd love to see the kind of man he grew into. Those eyes!" stated Faith with a gleam in her eyes.

"Arlon is missing, Faith. My daughter and I accepted the brief to investigate the events in the house next door because of our connection to it. That and the fact that our names keep appearing on the walls every night."

"You poor dear. How long has it been?"

"Six years."

"Hmm? Six years, you say? Why, that's about the time..."

"Yes, about the time all the trouble next door started. Not a coincidence, I don't think. If you ask our daughter, it's her father trying to communicate with us from the other..." Clarice had to stop herself before she gave too much away.

"From the other side? You believe he went to heaven and is trying to communicate with you?"

"No. Not only do I not believe in religion of any sort, but my husband also didn't die. He...went missing."

Faith wasn't sure what to make of the strange woman and her allusion. It didn't seem to make much sense: almost as though she was in denial. Faith thought it might be one of the stages of grief. A sudden thought about something the other woman said broke through her wandering mind.

"You said that your names keep appearing on the walls each night? Who puts them there?"

"That's exactly what we are here to find out."

"You mean you don't know? How's that possible?"

"Very much a mystery. For six years now the names Clarice

and Tara Blaze-Grey have magically appeared on the walls of the Bellows residence every night. Written in blood: human blood."

Faith Denham inhaled sharply and shuddered as though someone had walked over her grave. Paused in mid-air, the cup bearing the tea she was about to sip angled precariously as Faith contemplated the validity of the statement in the eyes of her guest. Only truth resided in those bright, clear eyes, making Faith feel all the worse. Before her tea spilled on the bright floral tablecloth, she straightened her back and regained control of herself.

"Can you think of anyone in the neighbourhood who might feel ill will toward the Bellows...besides yourselves, that is?" Clarice asked casually.

"How unkind of you to think I harbour ill will toward that poor family. You said yourself that it was my civic duty to report a suspected case of child abuse. That young girl looked a fright most mornings as she walked off to catch the bus down the road. I often said hello to her as she passed my yard," said Faith defensively, rising to clear away the dishes despite their cups remaining half full.

"I apologise, Faith. I didn't mean that the way it sounded. I don't mind admitting that this case is testing my patience and my skills. And I'm more than a little rattled by the tenuous connection to my husband. I was told that you'd had a bit of a run-in with Graham Bellows at some point and I based my rude assumption on that. Please forgive me."

There was a momentary pause in Faith's movements as she debated the sincerity of Clarice's apology. Intrigue about the events next door trumped her indignation, luring her to resume her seat with pursed lips to show her distaste at the accusation. Faith smoothed down the floral apron she wore over the floral print dress, ironed to within an inch of its life, as she descended. An awkward silence ensued as the two headstrong females contemplated the next round in the minor battle of wits.

"Faith, I'm a private investigator for an agency my husband and I started called the Bizarre and Mysterious Detective Agency. We specialise in the types of cases that regular law enforcement officers or private detectives would not normally consider. I investigate everything from the occult to the paranormal: all those things that are written about as fantasy or science fiction, from witches and possessions to ghosts and fantastic beasts.

"You'd be surprised at just how much business I have approaching me from all kinds of folks, some of whom are the least likely to seem the type. Graham Bellows saw my name in an advertisement I run in a magazine, after seeing my name appearing on his walls every night for six years. I was a Hail Mary, a last-ditch effort to come up with some answers for him. He didn't believe in ghosts and goblins, demons or saints. It pained him to call me. To invite me here to investigate.

"The events next door had driven him to drink, to the very edge of despair. That, and the nightly occurrences, drove his wife and child from their family home, causing untold hardship and suffering to them all. Julie Bellows fled the drinking and the cause of harm to her child, believing it was the only way to protect her daughter. Now that she has passed in gruesome circumstances, her daughter needs someone to care for her more than ever.

"Graham seems to have cut out the booze, at least temporarily, and I intend to complete my investigation because I don't think that young girl is safe. Something very serious and extremely dangerous is occurring next door to you, and I need to know anything you might know about, suspect or fear. I know I upset you and I did apologise for that, but, frankly, this is more important than your hurt feelings. A child's life hangs in the balance, making it bigger than you, me or even Graham."

CHAPTER FOURTEEN

It started around midnight with the familiar crack of deafening thunder, announcing another intrusion into their reality. The kitchen glowed with the ethereal, shimmering, blue radiance, bathing the frightened occupants with its menacing portent. The ceiling wavered with the pulsating flow of energy, undulating like an oily ocean at night reflecting the moon's glow.

Glunk, glunk, glunk.

The malevolent, pentrating sound bounced around the kitchen walls, causing the bile to rise in their throats, as the first sign of movement from beyond entered the halo of blue. The tentative approach of an unearthly hand extending through the circle of blue light made the small group hold their collective breath.

Glunk, glunk, glunk.

A true monster followed the hand through the aperture. No apparition, but a monster through and through, it twisted its loathsome head in every direction while the horrific sound continued. Unseeing, unfeeling, it rotated its gruesome visage in Clarice's direction, then the others in turn. The grey, leathery armour glistened with its sweat in the blue light. Observing in silent fascination, Clarice saw the creature open its almost perfectly round mouth, the razor-sharp canines extending from its maw in a menacing, circular, scything motion.

It became crystal clear to Clarice how the injury had been inflicted on Julie Bellows. It was a bite mark made by the horrific mouth she observed before her. The mouth opened and extended forward, slightly revealing the red/blue gums and those disgusting teeth. Clarice saw in her mind how the mouth would chomp down on its victim, rotate the teeth as it did at present, then gradually close its mouth, causing the teeth to almost meet at a point to remove a perfectly cone-shaped portion of flesh. The purpose behind such an act was not clear. How it benefited the creature caused Clarice to furrow her brow in consternation.

The noise continued for a few moments more, with no one breathing a word or making a sound. The creature seemed confused as it swivelled its grotesque head in every direction, making the dreadful sounds somewhere deep in its leathery throat that wobbled and bulged with the effort.

Gradually, the movement ceased and the sound abated. The hand and the head withdrew into the halo of light, which blinked out of existence without any of the previous chaos or fanfare. There was no warping wall, no exploding cutlery ejected from drawers, no electrical equipment whirring, whizzing or toasting.

Four exhalations were heard escaping the inhabitants of the kitchen as relief flooded through them.

"Okay, explain yourselves, young ladies, and it had better be good because I am totally freaked out right now," demanded Clarice in the sternest voice she could muster for someone as scared as she felt.

The pair of teenagers stood before her looking ridiculous in their suits of hand-crafted battle attire. Not that she and Graham appeared any less ridiculous for having been talked into donning similar garb made by the girls that day.

"It worked," squealed Tara suddenly, causing the adults to guard their hearing.

Cynthia joined in, grasping Tara's outstretched hands to dance in a circle, shouting in joy and triumph.

"Hold it, you two! What worked? What did you do and how did it work?" Clarice shouted in frustration, with just a hint of a smile forming at the corners of her mouth, as she felt just as relieved and elated as the girls.

Tara stopped suddenly. "Don't you see, Mum? *You* should. *They* don't."

"What are you blabbering about, Tara? They don't what?"

"See. They don't see, Mum. They don't have eyes. They use echolocation like bats to get around. It worked, they can't 'see' us because of our suits. I figured it out, Mum. The missing letters in those words."

Tara took a note from her pocket to show Clarice. "The words were 'Ɛ- G -- R- O- S SO-- D -- OO-- X-'," she announced each letter. "Egg cartons are the first two words, and sound-proofing is the second pair of words. That isn't technically correct; it's more like sound absorption. Bats use echolocation by sending out sound waves and listening for the echo as the sound bounces off prey or the geography around them. The egg cartons on top of the carpet absorb the sound instead of reflecting it."

"So the creature can't 'see' what it can't hear?" asked Clarice, with admiration for her daughter.

"That's right, Mum. If no sound is bouncing back at them from us, they don't know we're near. The sound they make is captured by the materials we're wearing. I know it looks stupid but it works! Daddy was right."

"Hold on! Daddy?"

"Daddy told me about it...sort of."

"Sort of?"

"I can't explain it, Mum. I just know that he communicates with me sometimes. I get pictures of words in my head without actually hearing him."

"So you went out and bought all this stuff, then spent the whole day making these...suits for us after hearing your missing father? You know how strange this is sounding, right?"

"It worked, didn't it?"

They were a sight, the four of them, standing in the kitchen of the riverside bungalow, dressed in bulging outfits of carpet and egg cartons. The relief in the air was palpable. Each of the occupants had a smile on the lips as they gazed at each other, feeling a little like survivors of a battle, when...

It startled the crew: a faint but distinctive cry from afar. Clarice recognised the voice instantly: a voice that was embedded in her memory, where it would never be lost to her. It was a voice that broke her heart to hear it, but she was overjoyed in equal measure. By the look on the faces of the other kitchen's occupants, they had heard the voice as well. Tears welled in her daughter's eyes at the familiar sound.

"Daddy!" she shrieked in excited alarm, turning every which way to discern the direction from which the voice had emerged.

"Clarice."

The voice became clearer. The direction was still obscured, but the natural timbre assured two of the onlookers who owned the voice.

"We're here, Arlon, we're here," whispered Clarice, barely daring to imagine she might be reunited with her man once more. Her tears flowed freely, as did Tara's.

The other pair watched the drama unfolding in fascination and bewilderment. Through Tara's calming touch, Cynthia had gained a hint of the magic the young woman had inherited from the energy encountered on their island misadventure. It awarded her a vision of the man Tara spoke of, her adopted father, Arlon Grey. Cynthia beamed with happiness for her new friend. Graham, without the benefit of shared minds, found the whole episode to be beyond bizarre and mysterious. He believed they were all headed for a mental asylum very soon.

A sudden crack of thunder outside the house startled them all. Clarice was the first to respond, waddling out of the house in her ungainly outfit, feeling like a version of the Michelin Man. She emerged into the night, unsure of what to expect. Moving from the bright blue lights, and then the ordinary fluorescent light when the portal collapsed, had shattered her night vision. All she saw were spots and stars before her eyes.

Before she had a chance to move forward, she was jostled aside by Tara, who was squealing with delight and excitement to see her father again. Their faces fell when their eyes adjusted to the darkness, with the spill of hallway light coming through the open doorway. The front yard was bare, with only the large realtor sign dominating the space. Joined by the others, Clarice and Tara searched the yard and street frontage desperately.

"A little help here?"

Clarice did a double-take when she saw a figure sitting above them on the roof. It was impossible to make out any details of the person beyond the bulky outfit, but the voice was too distinctive to belong to anyone other than the man of her dreams and heart.

"Arlon?"

"Who else?" he asked in a deadpan voice.

"Yep, it's him all right," said Clarice with a nod.

"Daddy!" Tara squealed again, rushing to stand below him with her arms stretched out.

"Who...who are you?" Arlon Grey asked in confusion.

CHAPTER FIFTEEN

The eyes were the same as she remembered. The enigmatic, crystalline, blue eyes, that drew in any female with their magnetism, had Clarice spellbound once more. They gathered in the annex of the caravan, sitting around a table, drinking a toast to the returned hero: non-alcoholic wine for all.

They had discarded their suits of ragtag armour against the sound demons. Arlon had still not heard an explanation of the girl who proclaimed to be his daughter. He was casting his eyes about in confusion, barely able to manage the changes in his wife. Although she was still the same Clarice he'd known, there were subtle differences that defied explanation in his mind.

Clarice had asked Tara to give the man some time to come to terms with everything, not wanting to overwhelm him. Tara tried her best to contain her enthusiasm and disappointment at not being recognised by her hero. Cynthia and Graham sat back to allow the family reunion to occur, enthralled by the appearance of the strange man wearing a uniform of some sort, reminding Graham of an old *Tarzan* movie he'd seen not long ago. He was happy for the woman and her daughter, but intrigued by the circumstances surrounding his disappearance and return. He held back on questions, however, while the small party ensued.

"Thank you for the reception, Clarice. Perhaps introductions might be in order?" asked Arlon in his blunt tone devoid of any emotion.

"Yes, of course. Where are my manners? This is Graham Bellows and his daughter, Cynthia. Folks, this is my husband, Arlon Grey."

Arlon shook hands with Graham and Cynthia, then turned to the young lady who had called out to him on the roof.

"And you are?"

"Don't you recognise your daughter, Arlon?" asked Clarice carefully, unsure if her husband was suffering some form of amnesia, perhaps from a head injury.

"Not possible. My daughter is only ten," explained Arlon patiently.

The sudden silence lengthened into an uncomfortable tension. Arlon peered at everyone intently.

"Arlon? Are you feeling all right?" asked Clarice.

"I'm fine, Clarice. Why do you ask?"

"You've been gone for over six years. Tara had her sixteenth birthday a few days ago."

"No. It's only been about six months since that night in the forest. It felt like years, but it was only... Tara Blaze-Grey? Is that really you?"

"Yes, Daddy. I've missed you...so much," said Tara, tears flowing down her cheeks.

She flung herself at Arlon, wrapping her long arms around his neck. Clarice also came around the table to hug her husband in a teary embrace. The family clung together for a long while as Arlon sat still with a look of stunned incomprehension. It was as close as he came to emotion.

"No, no, no, that will never do. I have to go back," declared Arlon, once he'd disentangled himself from Tara's clutches.

"Now just hold on there, bucko! You disappear for six years, then want to go back without an explanation or a by your leave? What gives?" asked Clarice, who had risen to stand with her fists resting resolutely on her hips, causing both Arlon and Tara to smile.

"I have missed you, wife," admitted Arlon sheepishly.

The blue eyes bore through to Clarice's inner depths, where she was slowly becoming unhinged. Her emotions warred with her as she fought to remain coherent before she ended up a blubbering wreck. Tara mirrored her pose as they both stared down at the man they loved in equal measure.

"Where the heck have you been for six years, Arlon Aloysius Grey?"

"You know you're in trouble when Mum uses all of your names," said Tara.

"Tara, is it really you? You look...you're a young woman now. I can't have it, Clarice. I missed out on that time. I have to go back, don't you see? To make it right."

"Make what right? Go back where? Make some sense, Arlon. Take your time and explain it to me," asked Clarice in a kinder tone as she resumed her seat.

"Would you like us to leave you all alone?" asked Graham respectfully.

"Don't you start! You stay right where you are, the both of you. We're all in this together now, so you'd better stay and hear what this is all about. Arlon, start talking, from the beginning," demanded Clarice.

"Six years? No wonder you look older and grey," Arlon blurted unintentionally.

"Well, thank you very much. Just what a woman yearns to hear from her long-lost husband. That time away certainly hasn't tempered your social skills. You're still a rude so-and-so. The story, bucko. Now!"

"Clarice, you know I didn't mean it like that."

"Skip it. Go."

"That night, in the forest? I felt the energy taking over, coursing through my body with a tingling, warming sensation. The next thing I knew I was travelling through some sort of vortex. I saw stars and planets whizzing by at incalculable speeds. I was being transported, for want of a better description, experiencing the path the meteor travelled. I was being whipped back through time, through alternate realities, through what I call an interdimensional wormhole. It was the opposite, though. I wasn't travelling; everything was passing by me. At least, that's how it seemed. I think...I think I was taken back to the origin of the asteroid, before the supernova of its sun

135

destroyed the planet from which it came.

"It was a primordial jungle of extreme volatility, with erupting volcanoes and tremulous earth movements constantly reshaping the topography. The journey then reversed, and I went forward in time to another destination, where I stayed for several days. It kept going like that until I learned to control the energy in me to stay put for longer periods.

"That asteroid reacted with its environment after it was ejected from the main body of the exploding planet. It crossed space and dimensions on its journey. Every phase of its path was replicated for me. I began to guide the energy within me, to find a better destination where I could practise the skill safely. I've seen... horrors you could never imagine. The moment I lose control of the energy, I get transported somewhere else. It took me quite a while to perfect the control.

"I ended up in a reality much like ours, at least, superficially. I popped out of the portal right in front of a humanoid creature that reached into the portal as it was closing and I stepped out. It severed the creature's hand. I used the energy in me to take away its pain and try to heal the wound. As the energy poured from me into the creature, we seemed to share thoughts and experiences. I found out more about them than I would've liked.

"The humans in that reality call the creatures the Guardians. They were the product of human genome experiments, in which they were spliced with animal DNA in a highly advanced society in a world where civilisation was nearly wiped clean by their advances. Pollution, climate change, diseases arising from those conditions: on and on it went.

"An elite faction rose to domination, restricted to a limited number of biospheres across the planet. The Guardians were manufactured to safeguard the elite and to farm the only remaining form of protein available to the ruling class, the less fortunate humans outside of the biospheres. Armed with an impenetrable layer of hardened skin, fingertips capable of injecting a neurotoxin from its reptilian genome, a form of echo location to hunt down prey on the darkened planet and underground where the rest of the humans fled, the Guardians were a formidable army with a type of hive mind. What one of them knew, they all came to learn.

"When I foolishly healed the injured one, it found out about interdimensional travel from me. I had imbued it with the same capabilities as myself and inadvertently armed them all with the knowledge of how to use it. The elite class had dedicated themselves to the pursuit of a new home, to begin again. They had been experimenting with wormhole technology to escape their time, to go back or forward.

"Through me, they learned of alternate dimensions: other planets and other realities where they could begin again. In the short time I was among them, I saw their thought processes change. I also saw and felt what the Guardians felt at the command of their masters. Instead of searching for a better place to begin again, they saw the opportunity to rule, to dominate less advanced civilisations. I have spent the last six months attempting to halt their progress by trying to locate and sabotage their machinery for producing continuum events."

Arlon took a moment to breathe heavily.

"How does all that tie into what's happening here, Arlon? Do you know?"

"Yes, I found out. They wanted exclusive access to the ability to travel between dimensions. Even though they had yet to master it as I had done, they were getting closer. They wanted not only to dominate their dimension and time, but all the others as well. To that end, I became a target in every dimension where I existed. In that reality, they searched and found this house I grew up in, hoping to kill me and anyone having anything to do with me. Their continuum displacement technology was not perfect. The attempted integration of dimensional and time travel was severely flawed.

"The intervals they enjoyed in other dimensions were very brief and often incorrect periods. They planned to kill me here in my past, when I was a child growing up, to be rid of the only other person capable of interdimensional travel. When that didn't work, they tried to lure you two here in the present as bait for me. Then they hoped to destroy you as well. You, Tara, because they knew you shared some of what I had."

"And me?" asked Clarice.

"Because of our child and the ability he would be born with."

"What child?"

"The one we haven't had yet. They've glimpsed the future and the past, Clarice, in multiple dimensions where we exist. Some of us are already gone from those dimensions. I couldn't save us. I tried as hard as I could to stay away from here, this reality, to keep them from finding it, from you and Tara. They used this house as a lure to get you here in the only time they could manage. They mean to wipe us out, anyone or anything that could possibly impede their road to domination."

"How did they do it, the names and then your messages?"

"They figured a way to write on the wall of this house in another dimension while employing the energy within them to transmute that writing to this reality. That way they could avoid entering the dimension until you showed up. I found the house and tried to do the same with my warnings, using my blood, in the hope you would have it analysed. I knew my DNA was recorded from my time with the force. It obviously worked."

Clarice and Tara nodded. "Who are they, these elite rulers?"

"Humans, or what becomes of us in another dimension after eons of evolution on a dying planet with depleted resources. Pure evil. If they perfect their devices and manage to kill off me, you and Tara, they will send the Guardians to destroy or enslave the rest of humanity here. The Guardians use the blood of their human prey to subsist, while the remaining meat is farmed and processed for the elite."

"And they want to do that here?" asked Graham.

"Everywhere. They plan to rule every dimension now that they know."

"The elite rulers that you say are humans, Arlon, how do they know what the Guardians found out?" asked Clarice.

"They can communicate with them somehow. I imagine telepathically, as the Guardians don't speak. It's all my fault, Clarice. That's why I have to go back, not only to set things back the way they were so that the Guardians never find out about other dimensions, but to set things right with us."

"I don't understand," said Clarice.

"I have to get back that six years."

"How on earth do you plan to do that?"

"By going back to access their time device, and *using* it instead of trying to destroy it. If I travel back to that forest before I get taken, I can reverse everything that's happened."

"I'm not sure it works that way, Arlon. Even if it does, what makes you think I want anything to change?"

"You mean you..."

"Oh, don't look at me like that. I missed you every day that you were gone, but I have a life I've lived with Tara for the last six years, none of which I'd be prepared to sacrifice."

"Clarice, you've seen them, the Guardians? You know how formidable they are. If the elite gets it all right, and they will eventually, it will mean the end of life as you know it on this planet in this reality. The non-elite in that other dimension are forced to live like animals, foraging and scrounging to survive in a darkened world, living mostly underground. If the elite figure out how to retain their Guardians here, without this reality reacting to them, it will be fatal for you all."

"Are you talking about the whole opposite thing? They can't exist in our reality without imploding like those creatures on the island?"

"Exactly."

"How did you survive that?"

"I was imbued with the energy from the meteorite or asteroid, or whatever it's classified as, that passed through that dimension and many more. Wherever that meteor went before it struck the earth to become a meteorite, I'm able to go without a reaction."

"You know this?"

"Theory. It's all a best guess, Clarice."

"And you can travel those dimensions at will now?"

"It takes an awful amount of concentration and energy on my part, but, yes. What I can't do is go back in time on my own. I need the device they use. I need to find someone in that dimension to help me get into one of the biospheres to access the machine and help me figure it out."

"So, *if* you find someone willing to assist you, and *if* you manage to get into one of their biospheres, and *if* you avoid whatever security they have, and *if* you find a way to make the machine work, which the highly advanced elite ruling group failed to do...?"

"I go back to that night in the forest. I train my past self to resist the energy's force to stay put. If I don't go into that other dimension, where I helped one of the Guardians, they won't know about us and everything is fine."

"Then there'll be the two of you here?"

"I...hadn't thought past that point. I suppose one of us will have to head off after that."

"To?"

"Another dimension?"

"Where you might come across another Guardian?"

"No, that..."

"It won't work, Arlon. You can't change the past and, as I said, I wouldn't want to change what I've had with Tara. I don't want to lose that."

"You wouldn't know about it, Clarice. I wouldn't vanish and life would continue from then as if none of it had happened."

"This is doing my head in. You folks can't seriously be talking about all this rubbish as if it's real?" insisted Graham. "I mean, other dimensions, asteroids, Guardians, time travel!"

"I'm all ears for your explanation, then," said Clarice. "My husband just returned after being gone for six years! That's a fact. He turned up immediately after we heard the crack outside, just as we've been hearing since we came here, through which those things, those...Guardians came. One of those things took your wife in front of your eyes, and you still deny this? You can spend all the time on the Egyptian river you want, Mr Bellows, but I think it's time you gave us the benefit of the doubt by allowing us to come up with some sort of plan to combat these things. In case you missed it, we're all in danger.

"I don't pretend to understand all of it, by any shot. Way out of my league and then some. I still have a lot of unanswered questions, but I think we've heard enough for now. Graham, I think you should take Cynthia and book into a cheap motel for the night. I'll foot the tab. Tara, I need you to go to bed, while Arlon and I catch up and see if we can come up with a strategy to combat these things without him having to disappear again."

Without much argument, everyone went about following Clarice's advice, albeit grudgingly, in Tara's case. After seeing off Graham and his daughter, Clarice and Arlon took folding camp chairs to sit outside the caravan annex under the stars, each with a glass of wine. Clarice was surprised to see Arlon drinking alcohol, something he'd never gladly participated in during their time together.

"Arlon?"

"Hmm?"

"Did you really miss me?" asked Clarice tentatively, fearing the answer.

Time seemed suspended as she watched Arlon struggle with a reply. It probably wasn't fair of her to ask him the question. The answer, when it came, shocked and pleased her.

"I didn't feel whole while I was away from you. There was an emptiness inside me that's only starting to fill again now."

"Thank you, Arlon. That's the most touching thing I've ever

heard you say."

"You'll have to store that up for when I'm gone again."

The sharp intake of air made Arlon turn to her. "I only came back to warn and prepare you. You're not safe as long as I'm here. I have to get back to that time device. Whether it works in theory or not, I have to try to make this better, Clarice. It's not just us we have to worry about, it's all the rest. I didn't know about the length of time that passed for everyone back here in this reality. I thought that missing six months after I disappeared wouldn't worry anyone too much. But, regardless of the increased time, I have to get back to that night if I can, to convince myself on that timeline, to train that person to resist the pull of the energy. If I never leave that forest, I don't save one of the Guardians and no one will be the wiser. This reality and every other one will be safe from them. Besides..."

"What is it?" asked Clarice, blinking back the tears.

"If the Guardians become ineffective in this reality, reporting back to their overlords about their failures, worse will come."

"Worse than the Guardians?" asked Clarice with growing concern.

"From what I can tell, the ruling elite are super intelligent and superior in technology in every way. When their world was dying, and crops were no longer possible, they came up with biospheres for the select few. They manufactured the Guardians to harvest the protein for them from the scavengers left outside the domes. They began working on a time device when it was clear that no other planet near them would sustain life. They theorised about going back in time to save their planet.

"I came along at an important time for them, when their time experiments were failing. In me, they discovered the possibilities of escaping to other dimensions, taking over, if necessary, from the occupants. They began ordering their Guardians to other dimensions, seeking ideal environments. You have to understand, Clarice, not all dimensions are populated with humans, or populated at all."

"How can you know all this?"

"Arlon Grey told me."

"Come again?"

"I searched out Arlon Grey in another reality. In that dimension, I still live in this house, which is where the Guardians tracked me down and found me. They managed to kill the other me, but not before he and I had long conversations. In that reality, Arlon Grey was a scientist, with a very jovial personality. He helped me piece together many of the facts and also came up with a lot of unproven theory."

"Wow, now there's someone I'd like to meet."

Arlon smiled sadly. "I know I'm not ideal, with my condition. Probably another good reason for me to leave you alone?" he offered.

"Sorry, Arlon, that was inconsiderate of me. Please don't think that way. I fell in love with you exactly the way you are and I wouldn't want you any different. Don't go."

"The Guardians and their overlords will stop at nothing to find a new home, and then begin their advance through every dimension until they rule them all. They are megalomaniacs of the highest order, Clarice, with technological abilities that will enable them to succeed. They'll find a way to combat the forces that prevent them from travelling through the portals at present."

"What's stopping them?"

"You saw what happened to any creature trapped in our reality on that island. Sooner or later they were exposed to the opposing forces, causing them to implode. It's positive meeting negative or worse. Like matter and anti-matter."

"Yet you survived," said Clarice.

"Yes."

"So...?"

"The overlords. They'll work out how to circumvent the opposing forces."

"They'll come here?"

"Once they find a solution, they'll travel everywhere. At the moment, only the Guardians, with their thick leathery armour, can survive for a short time. Arlon Grey, the scientist, thinks there may be a workaround solution for them. If they perfect the time device they may be able to travel back far enough to the source of the asteroid. If they can send back their Guardians to the planet before its sun goes supernova, they might be able to find the mineral within the planet that formed the energy. If they can bring that mineral back to their dimension, then they can possibly recreate what happened to me."

"And they know what happened to you because you saved the life of one of them?"

"Yes. The Guardians have been designed with many characteristics and qualities of the animal kingdom, including a hive mind. By sharing myself with one of them, and having that creature know my mind, they all know. Through my experience and practice with the energy, they informed their overlords who then used them to track me down...and you...and..."

"Tara? Arlon, I can understand why you stayed away so long, as twisted as that logic is to me, but you haven't taken something into consideration in all this."

"What's that?"

"You have a daughter who idolises you and loves you with every bone in her body. She never gave up hope that you'd return. She never grieved or felt your loss as I did, knowing that you would come back to her. If you leave again, you will break that girl's heart...as well as mine."

"Got that right," said a voice from behind them.

"Tara! You should be asleep, young lady."

"Really? Do you think I could sleep knowing Daddy is back? I've been tossing and turning all this time without a hope of going to sleep. I need to know what's happening. I'm invested in this as much as anyone," she pleaded.

Arlon and Clarice looked at one another in silent agreement.

"I can't get over how marvellously you've turned out, Tara Blaze-Grey. I can scarcely believe you're the same girl we rescued on that island only a year and a half ago...at least, that's how long it was for me. Sixteen? I missed it all. I never knew such a time difference was possible while I was away. Guess it has something to do with relativity. Go grab a chair and come sit with us, young lady. You're right, you do have a say in anything we decide. You might even be able to help us come up with a plan."

Tara rushed back into the annex to grab another folding camp chair. While inside she donned a light cardigan to ward off the cool early-morning breezes wafting in off the ocean. The family sat together in companionable silence for a few moments.

CHAPTER SIXTEEN

After speaking quietly until just before sunrise, the tired family group had trudged off to bed for some well-earned sleep. Emerging from the caravan into the annex much later in the day, Arlon inspected Tara's handiwork.

He nodded his head in approval at the design of the makeshift sound-prevention costumes she and Cynthia had made. The egg cartons and carpet had had the desired effect, just as he'd believed when he'd sent them the message. Arlon wasn't aware of how cryptic his message had turned out to be until he spoke to Clarice and Tara. He smiled at how clever his daughter proved to be the older she grew.

Arlon had listened with rapt attention to their story covering the six long years of his absence. If he could feel emotions, he would have been greatly saddened by their tale, knowing how they'd missed him and what he'd missed in return. It was a vast portion of Tara's life. To Arlon, only six months had passed since he'd last seen them in the dark, cold forest.

Admittedly, much had happened to him since then, none of it good. He'd been kept extremely busy and had not noticed the passage of time as acutely as his family had. Daily he had struggled with the decisions he'd made unilaterally to protect them. Those decisions were questioned by him incessantly, with only one obvious outcome; necessity proving them vital. The protective instincts in Arlon Grey were too powerful to ignore.

Never in his wildest dreams could he have imagined such events that befell him and his family, leading to his ride on an interdimensional roller-coaster, visiting parallel universes where other versions of himself existed. Arlon Grey had never so much as glanced at a novel in his forty-odd years of life, and would have thrown any book describing his adventures, if he had come across it, into the nearest bin. It defied his sensibilities despite all he'd seen and experienced with his own eyes.

It was easy for Arlon to understand the disbelief he had seen on Graham Bellows' face before leaving the gathering the previous evening. If he had heard such an incredible story he would have been twice as dubious and mistrusting.

Lost in his thoughts, Arlon was unaware that Tara was watching him with affection from the caravan door.

"They worked, thanks to you," said Tara quietly, not wanting to startle her father, a near impossibility.

"You did a great job. Considering the message was so garbled, I can't quite understand how you deciphered it, young lady."

"You sent me pictures, Daddy. I've always seen them and your words over the years. If I clear my mind and concentrate, I can see your face and your lips mouthing words to me. It takes me a while to work out what the words are, because the voice is mostly missing," said Tara, joining Arlon and placing an arm around his waist. "It's pretty strange to have you back again. How did you get on with Mum? Make any new brothers or sisters for me?"

"Tara Blaze-Grey!" exclaimed Clarice, her face bright red.

Arlon merely shook his head. "I think we were both too tired to even think about anything like that."

"Arlon! It's absolutely none of her business."

"We did just share a caravan, Mum. The thickness of a cotton curtain will not shut sounds out, you know?"

"Mind your manners, Tara. Besides...he doesn't even know about the addition to his family yet."

Arlon's ears pricked up at that. When no one was forthcoming with an explanation, he peered at Tara questioningly.

"Jarrah Bone," said Tara simply, as though it explained everything quite reasonably.

"Tara!" Clarice pleaded.

"There's a name I didn't think I'd be hearing again any time soon. I hope you aren't talking about us being the custodians of his bones or ashes?" asked Arlon with a furrowed brow.

"His offspring," said Clarice quietly.

"Maybe I'm being dense, but didn't you just say it was Jarrah Bone?"

"Come on inside while I make us a late lunch and explain," suggested Clarice.

Tara and Arlon climbed the steps back into the small van to sit at the dining nook. Arlon waited patiently for an explanation as Clarice prepared lunch for them.

"We named him Jarrah after his great-great-grandfather. We thought it would be appropriate for the love and respect Birrani bore his great-grandfather," said Clarice, with her back turned to Arlon.

"Ah, I see. Gloria Henderson?" he asked.

Clarice nodded. "She approached me about taking the child. She couldn't bear the sight of him: loathed him for what was done to her by his father. She'd hired a midwife when she found she was pregnant, delivered the child in absolute secrecy, and had a wet-nurse care for him. He was a toddler when she came to me, practically begging me to take him off her hands. Black as the ace of spades and big. Not as hairy as his father, thank goodness, but adorable."

"Not...deformed?" asked Arlon cautiously.

"Why would he be deformed?" she asked turning round to face him.

"Well, the father..."

"Birrani Nullah Bone was only deformed in the womb because of the abuse his mother suffered at the hands of that horrible man, Birrani's father. He wasn't some aberration formed from corrupted genes. Birrani's son is a pleasant and perfectly formed child only tending towards the same proportions as the black father and white grandfather. We thought of the name Jarrah to honour the man who took Birrani under his wing. I want to go back some day to find his relatives among the Gureng Gureng tribe, to find a suitable patriarch who can teach him the ways of his people in the same manner as his great-great-grandfather did for Birrani."

"You've officially adopted him?"

"Yes. The same man who helped us with Tara assisted us with all the paperwork to make it official. I didn't give him the name of Grey, though. I thought it best to retain only his tribal names unless he specifically asks for it when he gets older. He isn't the brightest of children, Arlon, but he's happy and loving. He'll develop in his own time."

"Well, well, well. I have a son I didn't know about after being away for just six months."

"Six years, Arlon! Jarrah is nearly eight," insisted Clarice.

"And he's where?"

"Staying with our next-door neighbour in Indooroopilly. She's been dying to look after him ever since we introduced him to her."

Clarice served them all a helping of scrambled eggs on toast with fresh coffee. They ate quietly, each lost momentarily in their thoughts.

"I smelled the coffee all the way over at my place. We came back from the motel earlier. I don't suppose I could grab a cup? We're out," explained Graham, poking his head into the annex.

"Come on in, Graham. Help yourself, there's plenty," said Clarice.

Graham entered the van. Discovering mugs hanging on a hook, he retrieved one and filled it to the brim with the exotic and highly aromatic blend. When he started to exit the van, Clarice stopped him.

"You don't have to go, Graham, unless you need to get back to Cynthia."

"I sent Cyn to one of her friends for the day. Being the school holidays, I thought it would be a good idea."

"Come sit with us, then. How did you fare at the motel? Get any sleep?" asked Clarice.

"Best sleep I've had in years, thanks. I feel like a new man. I..I haven't exactly been much help to anyone for a long time. I realise that now. You pushed a few home truths down my throat, which I guess I needed," said Graham with genuine regret.

"Happens to the best of us," suggested Clarice. "Right now, you have a daughter who will be depending solely on you to nurture her through the loss of her mother."

"What are your plans for bringing a halt to all this?" he asked Arlon.

Clarice rolled her eyes in frustration." Don't you go dismissing me all of a sudden, just because my husband turns up. *I* was hired to do a job and *I* will be the one to figure out what needs to be done...with Arlon's help, of course, but heading the investigation *I* started!"

"Whoa, no offence intended," declared Graham, his hands raised in mock surrender.

"Wouldn't pay to get on the wrong side of that little lady, Mr Bellows. She packs a mighty verbal wallop," warned Arlon with a grin.

"Yeah, don't dismiss my mum and me because we're female," added Tara unnecessarily.

"I'll thank you to butt out of my confrontations, young lady."

"I'm always saying the wrong thing to you, aren't I?" said Graham, screwing his face up into a comical frown.

"Yes. Seems you only open your mouth to change feet."

Graham grinned and nodded his head in agreement. "Okay, Clarice. What do you have in mind regarding our situation?"

"Was the writing on the wall again when you returned today?"

"No. Thank goodness. That hasn't stopped in a long, long time. This coffee is exquisite, by the way."

"Arlon's special blend," answered Clarice.

"You never stopped buying that particular blend from the Yarra Ranges?" asked Arlon.

"No, you spoiled us with that one. I tried to go back to an ordinary supermarket packet one week, and nearly spat it out in disgust at the first sip. It was awful waiting for the good stuff to arrive in the mail almost a week later. I stock up on it now and make sure I never run out. I'll give you the name of it and the ordering details if you like, Graham?"

"Thanks, but I don't think I'll be able to afford anything but off-the-shelf shortly. If I manage to sell the house, I may just have enough left over with the equity to purchase another house in the bush somewhere, but very little else. Maybe a rusted-up bomb to get around in. The realtor rang while I was inside and said he had a lot of interest in the house, but reports of our troubles are spreading and none of the interested parties are following through with requests to inspect."

"Perhaps I can help you there, Mr Bellows," said Tara.

"How so?" asked Graham, looking dubious.

"Once again you're being dismissive of a female. Or are you dismissing a minor?" warned Clarice fiercely.

"Sorry. I don't even know I'm doing it, if I am?"

"You are."

"Okay, let me reword that then. How might you be of assistance to me, Tara?" asked Graham, in the kindest tone he could muster.

"By allowing me to purchase your property...with Dad and Mum's permission, of course," said Tara brightly.

"I'm sorry? How's that possible?"

"Tara inherited a vast sum of money from her biological parents, which she gains access to on her eighteenth birthday. As her legal guardians and the executors of her trust, Arlon or I can advance funds for any projects or investments she requests before she comes of age, if we think it is worthy. I'm not entirely convinced that the purchase of your house would be an advisable or profitable course of action at the moment."

"I'm not thinking about it in terms of profit just yet, Mum. This is my Daddy's old house and I would like us to purchase it for him, for us, as a holiday home. If we bought the house, Graham and Cynthia could move away and get on with their lives while we work on solving the issues here," explained Tara with a beaming grin.

"What's this 'we' stuff? Regardless of what happens with the house, you will be going straight back to school after the holidays, young lady, in one week," said Clarice firmly.

"I could always..."

"Go back to school, just as I said," warned Clarice.

Tara looked to Arlon for support.

"Not sure why you're looking at me. I'm less convinced than Clarice about buying my childhood home. I have no fond memories of being here with my parents."

"Then why did you gravitate back there in that other dimension?" asked Tara with a look of satisfaction. "Why did you think your other self would be there?"

"I...I...can't answer that," said Arlon. "I suppose the location..."

"I think Tara's right, Arlon. It has to do with roots and our earliest childhood memories. You spent a portion of your impressionable youth here and probably feel this is home to you, despite your parents' best efforts to destroy that," argued Clarice reasonably.

"Mr Bellows and his daughter need help right now. Cynthia deserves a better life than the one she's known. You and Daddy need to fix the problems here, and the price of the house won't even make a dent in my inheritance. Please let me do this."

"I suppose you're going to want it at less than the bargain-basement price I've set it at, seeing as you know about the history?" asked Graham with drooping shoulders.

"Why are you asking me? Tara is the one who made the offer," said Clarice.

Graham reluctantly turned to her with a look of defeat.

"I know you have the house priced at below true value, Mr Bellows. I'm prepared to pay you the asking price. On top of that, if you haven't signed an exclusivity contract with the realtor, I can offer you a private deal, thereby forgoing the commission you would have to pay."

"How, how does someone your age know all this?" Graham

asked in bewilderment.

"My father and mother set me up with private tutors in business and economics from the age of ten to help me handle my inheritance when I turn eighteen."

"Nice to know you were listening in class," said Clarice with a proud smile.

"The market value for a house and land package this close to the river and beach will only rise over time. I can see it being worth twice its current value in less than ten years at the rate this area is expanding," declared Tara confidently.

"I will be happy to defer to your better judgement in that case, and offer my blessing and permission for you to proceed with the transaction, as long as the lawyers perform their full due diligence to make sure there are no hidden problems."

"Of course. Goes without saying. Daddy?"

"I don't think you need my permission as well. Only one legal guardian's permission is required, but you have it in any case. I don't think it will be a drain on your inheritance and I trust your business acumen when you say the value will rise. I've always trusted your decisions, Tara Blaze-Grey," said Arlon kindly.

"I know you have, Daddy. You and Mum always spoke to me like an adult and I appreciated it. Well, Mr Bellows, do we have a deal?" asked Tara, with her arm extended for the handshake.

"With one condition," he said solemnly.

"Which is?" asked Clarice apprehensively.

"If we shake on the deal, the house becomes your responsibility from that moment. Anything happening to the house, any damages, anything at all, falls on you. The sale stands and the problem is yours," stated Graham defiantly.

"That doesn't sound right to me," suggested Arlon. "Officially, the responsibility for the property only reverts to the new owner once the final payment is made and the contracts are signed."

"I know that. That's why I want it this way. You people are determined to stay here fighting this thing against my wishes. If you want the house it has to be under those conditions. Besides, I don't have insurance and couldn't cover damages. I don't have a pot to piss in any more. You insure the place the moment we shake hands or no deal."

"How would you have worked it with someone else looking to purchase your property, Mr Bellows?" asked Tara.

"It's a moot point. Nobody else will want the property because of the news stories. Tara, I know you're only doing this to help us out. What I'm asking is that you truly help us out. If you guys stay here, and something happens to the house as a result before the deal goes through, I'll be left with nothing at all. I can't afford the premiums or the exorbitant excess payment the insurance company will demand," Graham admitted with a reddening face.

"That will have to be up to my parents, then, as the house will have to be insured in their names while I'm still a minor," said Tara, turning to Clarice and Arlon.

"Your call, Clarice. I don't deserve a say after being away all that time while you handled everything on your own. Well done, by the way," said Arlon.

"You offered the deal and you'll have to finish it. I'll support whatever decision you make, Tara," said Clarice, pride causing her to shed a quiet tear.

"Then we have a deal, Mr Bellows."

Tara shook hands with Graham. The relief in the man's eyes was evident as he shook her hand for longer than normal.

CHAPTER SEVENTEEN

Contracts were raised and duly signed by all parties. Insurance was arranged in Arlon and Clarice's names. A substantial deposit was paid, building inspections were carried out, and due diligence was performed by a conveyancing lawyer. Graham and Cynthia found a place to stay out near Benaraby, where they would concentrate their search for a house to purchase.

A week had passed without incident since the sale of the house was raised by Tara, who was due back in Brisbane to resume her schooling. Phone calls were made by Clarice to ensure that Jarrah was being properly cared for by the neighbours. He spoke to Clarice and Tara in his childish manner, that bespoke of a slower than normal intellectual progression for a boy his age. Arlon was introduced to him over the phone, something he found unsettling.

Clarice noticed a silence about Arlon that exceeded his normal demeanour. Always thoughtful and quiet, he seemed overly concerned for a man without emotions. Clarice had to take him shopping in nearby Gladstone to purchase some new clothes for him. His favoured safari suit being unsuitable for their present situation left him with little choice in the matter.

Tara had taken an opportunity to say goodbye to her new beach-Beech-friend, whom she'd been seeing frequently over the preceding week. Clarice grilled her every time she returned, good-naturedly, though incisively.

Arlon and Clarice were sitting in the kitchen of their beach bungalow, courtesy of Tara's generosity. Clarice had spent days measuring windows and rooms, designing an interior that would suit their tastes, with Tara adding her valued opinions. The walls and cabinetry of the kitchen would need some serious attention after all that had occurred there. Apart from a few minor structural and aesthetic concerns, the building inspectors had found nothing else untoward or requiring extensive repairs. The new radio in the kitchen played an eighties tune softly in the background while they shared a coffee at the new kitchen table.

"Out with it," stated Clarice suddenly.

"Sorry, what?" he asked, startled.

"Whatever it is that has you quieter than normal, even for you."

"Clarice?"

"Don't go giving me those blue-eyed innocent looks that make me want to jump your bones. Come on, Arlon Grey, out with it. What's eating you?"

"A lot."

"Well, start somewhere."

"This isn't over."

"Never thought it was."

"I'm not entirely convinced with your argument that I can't go back in time using their technology to correct the mistake I made."

"That may or may not be true, but where does that leave us?"

"I don't understand."

"Arlon, you were gone six years last time. You say it was only six months for you. If you go back and it takes even longer, I may be nothing but bones when you return. You can't do that to us, especially not Tara. I don't think she could forgive you if you left her again. Not sure I could, either."

"I agree."

"Huh?"

"I agree. I couldn't ask you to go through that for me, either of you."

Clarice glared at him with worry churning in her stomach for what she believed the man of her dreams might be thinking. She armed herself mentally for the shock to come.

"Explain," she stated simply.

"You agree that this is far from over?"

"Certainly."

"You understand that I have to do something about it?"

"I understand why you think that."

"I'm the only one who can undo it, Clarice. If it isn't halted, this world, this reality, will fall victim to the elite rulers and their Guardians. You see that, don't you?"

"I see that they have to be stopped, yes. I see the imminent danger. I see that egg cartons and carpet will not stop this continuing. What I don't see is why Tara, Jarrah and I have to be the long-suffering martyrs left behind while you go off to fight for us all. It...isn't fair, Arlon. I...love you. I need you, and so do those children, even Jarrah, though he doesn't know that yet. I was hoping you could teach him the language of his people and so much more."

"Correct."

"What? Which part?"

"All of it."

"You're confusing me, Arlon. What are you saying...exactly?"

"I have to go back to make it all right if I can, and if my plan doesn't work I have to be there to find another way. That may take me years. At a ratio of 12:1: twelve months passing here for every month I'm there, I agree that it would be unacceptable for you and Tara. It would be for me as well, Clarice."

"So what are you saying?"

"That you have to come with me for us to stay a family."

"What!"

"It's the only possible solution."

"You can't be serious? How? No. How long? Arlon?"

"Calm down, Clarice, and think it through logically, just as I taught you. We agreed something had to be done. We agreed it had to be me. We agreed our family couldn't survive another protracted absence by me, and I admitted I would be reluctant to leave you behind. That leaves...?"

"Oh, this is too much. I think I need something stronger than coffee."

"It's going on lunchtime, Clarice."

"The sun's over the yardarm somewhere on the planet. I need something to steady my nerves. What you're saying is... well, it's preposterous and...impossible!"

"Which part?"

"Us...going with you. How would that be possible? Not that I'm thinking about it, mind you. Just humouring you at the moment. There are so many reasons for what you say to be pure fantasy and just...well...stupid! I can't begin to think of all the negatives about such a harebrained idea. You've finally flipped your lid, handsome."

Clarice rose to pour some wine from a bottle they'd opened the previous evening, which she'd enjoyed on the beach next to a welcome fire. Her hand shook as she poured the award-winning Chardonnay into the wineglass. With her back turned to Arlon, she attempted to relax. She turned suddenly.

"You could do it? You're saying you could do it?"

"I think so."

"Think?"

"I haven't exactly experimented with it, Clarice."

"So you want us to be your guinea pigs?"

"It would either work or it wouldn't. If it didn't work for you, then I would be gone only a short time before returning. We're talking minutes, not hours or days."

"Unless they were waiting for you there and prevented your return somehow, or..."

"Or?"

"Or killed you."

"I won't say that's impossible. There aren't any guarantees."

"But you're confident you can make it happen, aren't you? You wouldn't be suggesting it if you hadn't gone over and over it in your mind. That's why you've been so quiet, planning it all."

"Yes."

"You haven't even told me what it's like there. Are we going to come across the creatures we saw on the island? Are our lives going to be in constant peril?"

"Good grief, no. That was another reality altogether from the one I found where this house exists. Although it is somewhat peculiar in comparison to this reality, it is relatively benign."

"Let's say, just for the sake of it, that you could accomplish it and get us there, what then? Where would we stay? How would we live? It...it's all too much," said Clarice in exasperation, upending the glass and quickly refilling it.

"You might want to take it easy with the juice, Clarice. You don't handle alcohol very well, remember?"

"Says who?"

"Me. I seem to recall you had three glasses of wine and damn near attacked me once."

"I get randy when I drink, so what? You didn't fight me off or anything."

"Clarice! What if Tara heard you speaking like that?"

"Tara is sixteen years old, bucko, and knows what sex is."

"Doesn't mean we have to flaunt it in front of her," he replied weakly.

"You can't get embarrassed, and I don't mind that she knows we love each other enough to have a healthy sex life. Stop getting off the subject. Answer my questions and leave the drinking to someone who knows how to enjoy it."

Clarice sat back at the table and glared at him defiantly.

"Well, we'd live *here*."

"Thought you said we'd be going to that other dimension?"

"Yes."

"Huh?"

"This house in the other dimension," he explained simply.

"Oh! Well, then. Clear as mud! Don't you think the owner would have something to say about a strange family moving into his house?"

"Well, technically, I would be the owner."

"Arlon, we bought this house, here, with Tara's money, not at the other place. Right?" she asked, uncertainty causing her brow to wrinkle.

Arlon peered at his wife with something resembling amusement and affection. No one was capable of moving him as Clarice could. In bed, she was a wanton woman, a veritable tiger without inhibition. In other situations, she was an indomitable force, immovable if she dug in her heels about some issue and decided she would not be swayed. Arlon had never met another person capable of reaching into him to produce anything like an emotion.

"Clarice," he explained kindly, "in the other dimension, Arlon Grey owns his childhood beach home. He was assassinated by the Guardians in that dimension. If we went there, I would be taking his place, in effect. As for his living, he was a scientist, as I mentioned, with some very profitable patents to his name. We would be relatively well-off in that reality. His wife died of cancer and he fathered no children. Might have some explaining to do to the neighbours, if they knew him, but that's it."

"If those things killed you...him...there, that means it isn't safe."

"We aren't safe here. We aren't safe anywhere until I fix things. They'll find me, us. They can home in on my energy across the parallels, across time and space. They will always be able to find me because of that meld that occurred."

"Oh, Arlon. I love you, I really do. I missed you so much that I truly believed I was going to die of heartbreak at one point. Only Tara kept me from sinking into an abyss. What you're asking, though...even if you're capable of getting us there... how long would we be there? When would we come back?"

A long silence ensued. Arlon fixed his deep blue eyes on Clarice; her eyes bored into his. It was some time before she understood. She nodded sadly. "We can't come back, can we?"

"I don't think so, Clarice. I expect we will be away for two to three years, at least, trying to sort it all out. That means somewhere between 24 and 36 years will have passed here, using the 12:1 time differential ratio. If we leave, it will be for good, not only to keep this reality as safe from the Guardians as possible, but because this world we know will have changed so much that we may never again fit in. Who knows what climate change or war will do to this world while we're gone. Banks and economies may collapse, leaving us destitute, with no home to return to.

"I know this is a hard choice for you, Clarice. I *have* to go. You don't. Whichever way you decide, I'll support your decision."

"Do you love me, Arlon?"

"As far as I know, yes."

"That doesn't inspire confidence in me."

"I have no emotions, Clarice. They're foreign concepts to me. I can't feel loneliness, but I know how empty my life seemed without you and Tara in it. I have never been intimate with another woman, so I have no point of comparison, but I know I have never *wanted* to be with anyone else. I respect and admire you for everything you are and everything you do. I wouldn't want to change a single thing about you, regardless of our huge differences in...everything! I have alexithymia, Clarice. I am autistic and, as such, will never be capable of providing that romanticised notion of love that you read about in novels or see in the movies.

"I can only offer you everything I am. When I married you I promised to give you my protection, my fidelity, my best efforts to keep a roof over our heads, wholesome food in our bellies and, when we were ready...a child. I have never wavered in those promises...except for leaving you alone for so long, something I had no control over at first. I told you a long time ago that you shouldn't hope for changes to occur in me. I will never know or express joy. I will also never know anger, jealousy or any of the negative emotions associated with inharmonious relationships. I asked you once if you were prepared to accept all that if we were to be married. You replied in the positive. Has that changed?"

"N...no. No, that hasn't changed. I'm a little older and wiser since then, perhaps, and some of my priorities have changed."

"That's only natural when a child comes along. It's also perfectly understandable when you are suddenly thrust into motherhood alone. Please understand that I had no way of stopping what happened at the time. I wasn't able to control that energy as I can now. Once I learned to control and manipulate it, I was placed in the position of staying away to protect you and Tara from the terrors I encountered."

"I get that, Arlon. But this is a little overwhelming, so bear with me, okay? There's no rush for a decision, is there?"

When Arlon did not answer immediately, Clarice gulped another mouthful of wine. "Why are we in a hurry?"

"The elite humans are technologically advanced, Clarice. It won't take them long to find a way of protecting themselves and their Guardians from the effects of displacement in a foreign reality. Hell, a simple suit of some kind might fit the bill, and they'll be here with their advanced weaponry before we know it. I came up with a suit of sorts, made from nothing but rubbish, to throw off the Guardians. I have to get them away from here to protect this realm."

"Who protects us and the realm we travel to?"

"I do, to the very best of my ability...with your invaluable help. Tara, too."

"What about bug-a-lugs?"

"Hmm?"

"Jarrah Arlon Bone."

"You, you gave him my name?"

"I did."

"That was very thoughtful of you. Not sure I deserve the honour, though, seeing as I've had no input into his life to date."

"You saved his mother...and his father, for that matter. I'd say that was enough input."

Arlon gave Clarice one of his rare smiles.

"He'll have to join us, then," said Arlon simply.

"It's a long journey back to Brisbane. I suppose if we pack today we can..."

"That won't be necessary. Tara and I will go and pick him up when she comes back from the beach. I assume she and Jarrah get along well together?"

"Two peas in a pod, those two. Why will it take less time for you and Tara to travel to Brisbane than all of us?"

"I need Tara because Jarrah will recognise her and most likely not put up a fuss. With our 'shared' abilities, it will take less time to condition her for the type of travel I have in mind. It will take me far longer and, most likely, exhaust me to apply that conditioning to you. You'll probably resist my influence, as well, knowing you."

"You calling me stubborn?"

"As a mule," he replied with a smirk and twinkle in his eye.

"How do you plan on getting Jarrah back here that way?"

"He's young and, according to you, not operating on the same intellectual level as most kids his age? If that's true it shouldn't take much for me to implant the skills he needs to travel with us. Going there will be instantaneous. Getting back will take a few hours while I recuperate from the exertion. Back in time for dinner?"

"Then what?

"You."

"Me?"

"Hmm-mm."

"You make that sound like it'll be a trial."

"You have trust issues."

"I do not."

"And stubbornness."

"Not!"

"Mulish and dogged resistance to almost anything that challenges your independence."

"You're wrong."

"And obviously capable of self-denial lately?"

CHAPTER NINETEEN

Cyclone!

At least, the other world equivalent of a cyclone lashed the shores of the beach, whipping the waves into a frenzied froth. The shutters of the beach bungalow belonging to Arlon Grey, inventor and eminent scientist, were tightly closed, but a CCTV view displayed mother nature in her full fury to the group gathered in the main living room.

Jarrah's eyes were wide as saucers as he huddled between Clarice and Tara on the settee. Arlon sat beside them in the armchair with a steaming hot cup of his favourite brew. He'd taken great pains to ensure a goodly portion came with them on their journey, wrapped in natural hemp to withstand the process. His recollections of the coffee available to him in the other dimension were enough to convince him to be prepared.

The process of training Tara for transportation to Brisbane, then gaining the boy's confidence sufficiently to instil the energy in him and train him to use it, then training Clarice, had taken almost a week. Nothing untoward had occurred during that time, worrying Arlon more than he let on. While the tempest raged outside their new home, Arlon considered the reasons for a lack of visitations by the Guardians or their masters.

It seemed to Arlon that no news was not good news in that scenario. It meant the masters were intent on devising methods to cross the thresholds themselves. With the masters acting as eyes for the Guardians, no one would be safe. Every moment in their old dimension drew the danger nearer to them and the rest of the world. It was a great relief when he was finally able to prove that he could do as he'd forecasted.

With Tara safely transported to the other reality in Arlon-the-scientist's home, he grew confident that he could repeat the actions with the other two. It took him and Clarice working together to influence the mind of the young boy. He was too young and a little too slow to fully comprehend the vagaries of the energy. Arlon and Clarice had to take over his mental functions, essentially.

Their entrance into a catastrophic maelstrom had been an unpleasant and frightening experience for the children. Thankfully, Arlon had managed to transport them to the front door of the beach bungalow. He dared not open a portal within the house for fear of destroying it if opened on a structural beam or the like. It was not an exact science, by any means; it was all done by feel and memory.

Arlon was able to travel to any destination in space or dimension through which the asteroid had passed. The historic journey, covering many millions of years, led through innumerable realities and unexplored space. Arlon's backward journey through everything in a fraction of the time, allowed him access to it all if he chose.

Unfortunately, that also meant the Guardians had access to it all. Not only did the Guardians share that ability, due to a hive mind mentality, probably genetically spliced into the new DNA, but their masters were also toying with time travel and succeeding, to a certain extent. Perfecting that mode of travel would not take the masters long, according to what Arlon knew of them.

At Arlon's last count, he estimated the masters' Guardians had succeeded in dominating at least half a dozen suitable worlds in the short period of six months that he had been away. Several different versions of himself from those dimensions had been assassinated by the Guardians. They were relentless in their pursuit of him. He sensed whenever they were closing in on him. Then he would hear those horrible glunking sounds which would have made his skin crawl if he had any emotions.

He did not have a plan for battling the masters when they arrived in whatever protection they'd developed to allow them to survive the dimensional displacement. It was Arlon's theory that any being outside their dimension would be subject to their opposite energy. If that opposing force managed to meet any internal part of a biological being, it reacted explosively. Although the theory had yet to be proven scientifically, something their current world's Arlon Grey had been working on before his untimely demise, it seemed to play out in practice enough to satisfy Arlon.

He might have proved his theory, in any case. Arlon and, subsequently, Tara, Clarice and Jarrah, had been instilled with the energy he'd received. That energy protected them from the same consequences of interdimensional reactivity. Unfortunately, that flew in the face of why the Guardians were not protected as he and his group were.

Tara, Clarice and he had been subjected to the energy directly to varying degrees, Arlon's exposure being the longest and most intense. Jarrah had only an indirect or second-hand connection to that energy through Arlon, yet he suffered no adverse reactions to the new dimension. Arlon was very careful to monitor the boy's chemistry during the transference.

The Guardian whom Arlon had saved experienced that same second-hand exposure to the energy, which it passed on to its brethren. They were not protected, for some arcane reason that Arlon could not discern, other than to assume it had something to do with their unnatural genomes.

Clarice told him about the hand of the Guardian which was lopped off by the closing portal, exposing the inner flesh and bones to the opposing dimension, causing it to react explosively. Their tough, leathery skin protected them for short periods only, much like the furry, purple, dog-like creatures they'd encountered on the island, whose thick fur matting had kept them safe for a time.

"So no money?" Clarice asked, disturbing his train of thought.

"Um, no, not as such. Everything here, all transactions, worldwide, are made on a bartering basis for credits. Everything is valued by a global market authority and transaction house which monitors all transactions for a percentage of the value. Something similar to crypto-currency, maybe?"

"How the heck am I supposed to do shopping like that?" asked Clarice, shouting above the roar of the strengthening wind.

"How do you do shopping normally? You use money, right?"

"Yeah, so?"

"What's money?"

"Huh?"

"It's nothing but paper or plastic, right? Those notes represent a unit of value. That value enables you to purchase items of equivalent value. You trade a piece of paper or plastic for a vegetable, say, or a bottle of milk. You are exchanging a note with a perceived value *only* for a real item. You couldn't pay for that item with a piece of paper you tore from a notebook, for instance. It's bartering, as well, only with physical representations of value. Here you have nothing physical to carry around with you, other than the wrist-mounted device that stores the digital information about your current holdings in the form of credits. It is, essentially, no different to waving your mobile phone over an EFTPOS device to make a cashless transaction back home."

"How will I know how much something will cost?"

"Everything is priced in credits the same way as home, Clarice. Why are we talking about this during a cyclone?"

"Because I'm bloody scared, Arlon, and talking about mundane shit like that takes my mind off dying, okay?" Clarice shouted.

"You want to go down to the bunker?"

"This house has a bunker?"

"Sure."

"And you only tell me about this now?"

"I think we're perfectly safe up here, Clarice."

"You think? Arlon, we have children here who are probably even more scared than I am. Get moving, bucko!"

Arlon led his little troupe along the hallway, Stopping at a hall runner, he lifted the end of the rug to reveal a trapdoor in the wooden floorboards. Raising the trapdoor exposed narrow stairs leading to a brightly-lit concrete bunker set up with all manner of scientific equipment. Electronics, chemistry vials and flasks, beakers of every size and description, were scattered over numerous stainless steel benches.

Clarice turned in dismay toward Arlon, who was closing the trapdoor behind them, effectively reducing the noise of the storm to negligible levels. "Arlon, is this stuff safe around the kids?"

"Keep going forward into that next room. The other Arlon had it set up comfortably, like a liveable den. All mod cons. I recommend that no one touches anything at all in here."

Clarice herded the two children into the cosy-looking room next to the laboratory, which included a foldout sofa bed. It was getting toward 10 pm in the new dimension. They had left their reality at around ten in the morning, so were all suffering a type of interdimensional jetlag: not tired, but weary from tension and the mental process of transference. Clarice and Arlon unfolded the sofa bed so the kids could lie down while they waited for the storm to abate.

Arlon managed to find some wine to help ease Clarice's nerves. Although dog-tired himself from the mental exertion, he was indifferent to the tensions everyone else was feeling. At times, he truly appreciated that he was unable to feel emotions like the rest of humanity. Having only ever experienced them while under the debilitating influence of the energy when he first encountered it, he had no desire to return to that state. Keeping his persona to a sustainable equilibrium had served him well his entire life. He had no use for all the pitfalls associated with human emotions. A logical and enquiring mind was all he required to be content with his lot...if he could feel contentment.

"Is this weather normal here?" Clarice asked.

"Is weather normal anywhere?"

"That's not an answer, Arlon Grey."

"What's normal, Clarice Manning-Grey?"

"Touché."

"We had cyclones in Queensland, droughts in some areas, dust storms in the central regions associated with those droughts, hail in the eastern regions, icy blasts on the highlands. Weather is unpredictable no matter where you are, Clarice. I can see where this is heading and you might want to stop yourself."

"And where do you think this is heading? Whatever 'this' is."

"It's only natural that you might start making comparisons and finding things not to like about this place, Clarice. That won't help anyone settle in, least of all those two."

"It's different, Arlon," Clarice explained earnestly.

"Certainly."

"And?"

"And nothing. It's different. So what? We learn to adapt."

"It's not like moving to another state or even another country. They don't even have money here. What else haven't you told me about this place?"

"Credits are just another form of currency, Clarice. Sure, there are many different things here, not all of which I know about yet. Would you know everything there was to know about Thailand if we'd moved there? Or China?"

"We aren't talking about anything as simple as that, Arlon. We're talking about another...planet! They don't even speak English here, and certainly not with anything resembling an Australian accent."

"Of course not. We aren't in Australia."

"See? Where are we, then?"

"Same geographical location on the planet, just not inhabited by Australians. It hadn't been discovered by Captain Cook in this reality. The equivalent of the Spanish discovered it here. They speak an odd sort of Lingua-Franca, a mixture of languages that we will all have to learn eventually. However, the eminent scientist, Arlon Grey, has a translating device which he made especially for me so that we could communicate. I'll see about getting us all one to carry around with us. Has to be some way of reproducing or copying the device if it's reverse-engineered by someone."

"You never told me we'd have to learn another language! How the heck is Jarrah going to cope? He's having difficulty enough with English."

"Not too late to go back, if that's what you're hinting at," said Arlon in a neutral tone, so frustrating for most to hear.

"Could we?"

"Certainly."

"But not you?"

"No, I would have to return here, not only for our world to survive, but to protect this world as well."

"What's so special about here?"

"You'd be surprised. There is a unified world here, one of relative tolerance, governed by a global body, an overseeing entity to which all countries are held liable. It has a global currency and overall laws that are uniform in nature, with only minor differences attributable to varying ideologies. It isn't a democracy as such and not quite communism; it falls somewhere between. The leaders in the global entity are chosen for their expertise, not their popularity, and are all paid a flat, low rate for their services. Local elections are held for the council positions covering all departments, such as health, law, infrastructure, etc... Those elected officials place qualified personnel into a ruling body above them, dealing with federal and global matters. Representatives from that body are promoted to the global entity on merit for a fixed term of ten years. It provides for stability and reliability across the globe. Every country has a say in everything that matters. The checks and balances within every government are considerable, making corruption very rare.

"That's not to say that crime or problems don't exist here. However, there haven't been the world conflicts that we've had. No holocausts, or Hitler, or other dictators in third-world countries that have stripped their economies bare or ripped off the assets. There have been no great famines or plagues. If something happens in one country, such as drought, there are measures in place to deal with it by the governing global body. There is greater control and sharing of resources overall. I may be painting too altruistic a picture, but it does seem to work better than our system of government."

"You like it here?"

"I can't like or dislike, Clarice: you know that. Logically, this place works better than ours, that's all. Is it worth saving from the Guardians and their masters? Absolutely! Plus, I have a certain investment, a reason to make amends here."

"The other Arlon Grey?"

"Yes. I feel I owe it to him after he helped me."

"It must have felt really weird talking with yourself."

"It wasn't me I was talking to. He only looked similar to me. Personality-wise, we were worlds apart."

"Ha, bloody ha! I see your attempts at humour are still woeful. Don't give up your day job...which you don't have anymore. How well off are we here?"

"No one is truly destitute here unless they are bone lazy or criminally minded. It's pretty hard to be unemployed unless you wish to be. There aren't any social payouts for the unemployed unless there's a legitimate medical reason. Even the voluntarily unemployed can receive food from handy soup kitchens set up by the local councils. They use up all the leftover food from restaurants and hotels. There are significant fines for any business caught wasting edible food by throwing it out. So no one goes hungry here, no matter what. The homeless are well fed: not that many are homeless for long."

"What about the handicapped?"

"There aren't any. Genetic engineering ensures defects are eliminated. Accidental paralysis or damage to eyes, ears and every other organ is repairable or replicable here."

"Replicable?"

"As in new ones, yes."

"New organs, how?"

"Grown artificially, commercially."

"New limbs as well?"

"Correct. Medicine is far advanced here and highly effective at eliminating all manner of maladies."

"What about the problems of the older generation, such as dementia, for instance?"

"Eliminated."

"Wow! How long do people generally live here, in that case?"

"Average life expectancy is around 150."

"That would mean serious problems with overpopulation, wouldn't it?"

"Ah..."

"What?"

"Well, I mentioned that there was better control over some things here. Population stabilisation is one of those. If any area or country is experiencing a burdensome birth rate it is effectively controlled."

"Involuntary birth control?"

"Yes and no. The laws were voted on and are carried out accordingly. Everyone knows about the law, yet they have no way of knowing if it's being applied to them."

"How is it administered?"

"Through the air and the water. Once a suitable level of population growth for that region has been stabilised, the control is rescinded."

"Big Brother?"

Arlon nodded. "Or else you can look upon it as free birth control for countries in which their people are less inclined to worry about such things," Arlon suggested. "The people know about it. Nothing is hidden from them 'for their own good' and all that rubbish. It isn't perfect here, Clarice. Better, I would say, but far from perfect. I haven't brought you to Utopia, if that's what you were thinking."

"You still haven't discussed with me how you're going to go about saving the human and other species in multiple realities."

"I still believe that going back in time is the best possible solution. I have to go to their home world for that."

"Not that I'm agreeing with your plan, because I can't, but is there a time difference between that world and this?"

"I don't know. That's why I have to test it before I spend a long time there. We'll synchronise watches before I leave. I'll only stay for one hour, then we'll compare our watches on my return. If the time's out by a few seconds, I won't be concerned. Anything over a few minutes could be worrying."

"Then what?"

"If a notable time difference is not evident, I proceed with my plan to break into one of their biospheres. I locate their laboratory, then force one of their scientists to teach me how it works. I go back to the night in the forest and warn myself. No, *teach* myself how to control the energy to avoid vanishing."

"What do you expect to happen after that? With us, I mean?"

"Complicated and purely conjecture."

"To the best of your knowledge, then."

"Well, here's what I hope. I go back to that night. Arlon...'junior' learns how to avoid vanishing and I return to the realm of the Guardians briefly. The three of you from that period, that reality, go about your lives as if my vanishing had never occurred. I have removed us from their future. One of two things could happen after that. Either we simply vanish from here to resume our life six years after I disappeared, or..."

"Or?"

"We don't."

"Jeez, Arlon. What does that mean?"

"If we change the past, it affects the present and the future. That's my theory, anyway. Plenty of scientists disagree. If I manage to succeed in training Arlon to avoid his disappearance, I may well disappear there and then. You, Tara and Jarrah will also vanish from this reality. We all go back to the time it was before we came here, only..."

"Only?"

"Only I have no way of knowing what happened to us in the new history of the elapsed time our family spent between being in the forest and when Graham Bellows contacted you. It will be an entirely new set of experiences for us all, if we're even together, that is. A lot can happen in six years. One of us could have become ill or had an accident, or any number of other things might have happened.

"Then, again, it may be that I will remain behind once the other Arlon learns to avoid vanishing, and I return here to find you all exactly as I left you. The reason that may be a possibility is that I removed us from the original reality we just came from. Our present selves may not be affected because we are currently in another dimension."

"Well, you were right about one thing, bucko!"

"Which is?"

"It's bloody complicated."

CHAPTER NINETEEN

The time difference was negligible: a few seconds. Arlon could spend days or a month in the world of the Guardians and their masters without an appreciable difference from their new reality. They had experimented with it a dozen times to be 100% certain. It was the same proportional result whether he stayed away for an hour or a day.

When Arlon made the final journey to the home world of the Guardians, he was dressed in his ridiculous egg carton and carpet outfit. The perpetual semi-darkness of the Guardian world meant he had to be extremely careful to watch every footfall. The planet was dying and the sun was shielded by a heavy layer of industrial smog overhead, causing the landscape to take on an eerie effect. The site at which Arlon had transported himself was where he'd encountered the Guardian on his first sojourn through the dimensions, following the path of the asteroid before it plunged into earth and was eventually reclassified as a meteorite.

It was clear that Arlon had inadvertently caused the creature harm. He did not hesitate to assist. Placing his hand on the body of the unclothed monstrosity, Arlon felt their minds melding and saw the memories of the Guardian and its brethren. The insect genome spliced into the human DNA was more than likely from ants, bees or whatever the equivalent was in that reality.

The information he received in the mutual bond left him reeling. If he were able to display disgust and revulsion, he would have let loose with it then. The hive mind revealed the barbarity of their duties, to defend the masters and provide for them in a world devoid of soil capable of sustaining crops or grazing animals. The feral humans left to roam the toxic planet outside the domes subsisted on a type of algal bloom that exploded in still water. The algae did not require the sun, using a geothermal synthesis instead of photosynthesis to multiply and survive when everything else failed.

A plethora of information was gleaned by both parties in the exchange between Arlon and the injured Guardian. The information extracted from Arlon was related to the masters by the Guardian. How that exchange was carried out wasn't clear to him. The Guardians seemed to communicate telepathically, as far as he knew, being without eyes and ears, from what he could see. They navigated by way of echolocation, as bats do. They used that to perfection to hunt down feral humans living mainly underground to avoid the topside pollution.

Arlon assumed that the genes of a reality-equivalent vampire bat were used in the genetic coding of the Guardians. Witnessing first-hand the method by which the Guardians fed left no doubt in his mind about the assumption. A Guardian would hunt its prey and inject the feral human with a neutralising, anticoagulant venom secreted from their pointed fingers. Within moments, the victim would cease all movement, allowing the predator to remove a conical-shaped piece of flesh from the prone figure.

The Guardian would suck the blood that pooled in the cone reservoir formed from the bite until the body was dry. It would then transport the corpse to the biosphere, where it would be processed into palatable protein bars for the masters to eat with their vegetables grown within the domes under artificial light. It was a symbiotic existence for the masters and their Guardians.

The Guardians were reliant on the masters for a life-sustaining enzyme injection, without which they would last only a day or two. Without the Guardians, the masters were defenceless against the hordes of feral humans outside the domes, always seeking ways to penetrate the walls in the hope of destroying them. The domes were insufficient in size to allow grazing animals, and had no means of growing stock feed to sustain them. Real estate was at a premium, which the masters were not willing to compromise while perfectly good protein was available in plentiful supplies outside their enclosures. Cannibalism wasn't unheard of in earth's history, so Arlon wasn't at all surprised to find it in the new reality, where farming was no longer a possibility outside the domes.

A gas mask was required if someone found themselves outside the domes for extended durations. The Guardians, maybe designed to withstand the toxicity, did not require that precaution. The feral population grew to withstand the toxicity in short doses, but those exposures caused gross abnormalities in their offspring. Mutations, or 'mutes' as they were called by the masters, could stand more of the topside air than their parents, so it was left to them to scrounge about topside for anything that might assist in survival and to harvest the algae.

Mutes and feral humans spoke in mere grunts and used hand signals to prevent them from opening their mouths too much while exposed. Their language was nearly impossible for Arlon to decipher and use. The masters, however, had developed a highly sophisticated language that Arlon had gleaned a moderate understanding of after only a short time listening to one of them. The gift of languages came to Arlon more easily than most. In his reality, he had mastered over 100 different languages, including many aboriginal dialects.

The only reason Arlon could listen to a master was the presence of a defector living outside the biosphere, whom he had stumbled across the first time he'd found himself in their reality. Bufta was as close as Arlon could come to pronouncing his name in an anglicised manner. After spending a few days in Bufta's presence, Arlon had picked up the essentials of the language enough to hold a basic conversation with the male master. Surprisingly, Bufta had shown remarkable advances in picking up English from Arlon.

The masters were an effete race of humans varying in physical attributes in the same manner as any humans. Although their mannerisms and speech were reminiscent of the French or English aristocracy during the middle ages, effeminate and rather insipid as a whole, Arlon observed, it was easy to see why they required the army of Guardians to serve and protect them. Intelligence they had in spades, but courage and physical prowess they lacked considerably. Bufta was an exception, standing at over 180 cm, with a powerful build. Possibly it was that distinction that drove him from the biospheres when he was unable to form friendships among the snobby elite.

It was toward Bufta's underground home that Arlon travelled through the murky, dismal atmosphere. A constant low-lying fog covered the dead forest through which he walked, with gnarled and bare trees poking through the mists every few metres. The ground was relatively even despite many domiciles existing beneath the earth, their entrances hidden as much as possible from the prying penetrations of the dreaded Guardians.

The distinctive glunking sounds made by the Guardians could be heard by Arlon in the distance. Hoping he was concealed sufficiently within his cloak of sound-absorbing materials, Arlon kept up his medium pace to reach Bufta's hideout in the low hills a mere two kilometres from the western wall of the planet's main biosphere. With a radius of five kilometres, it meant the area within the dome measured roughly 78.54 square kilometres, according to Arlon's maths, using the simple formula $A=\pi r2$.

Knocking four times, pausing, then knocking three more times elicited the response he was hoping for from the inhabitant of the secret grotto. The door was hidden within the trunk of a dead forest giant and disguised to resemble a continuation of the tree's interior with the bark removed. There were no visible handles or hinges on the exterior. Only Bufta knew the sequence of pushes and taps required to release the mechanism from the outside.

The hidden spyhole, secreted within a natural knothole, slid open enough for the occupant to peer outwards. Had Arlon not been made aware of the peephole, he would never have guessed it was there. The sound of the many locks and latches being sprung from behind the solid door caused Arlon to frown. If Bufta were being chased by a Guardian, Arlon did not think he would escape if it took so long for the door to open.

Cautiously, the door edged outward, another safety measure. Bufta had ensured that the door could never be forced inwards against the metal jambs framing it. The rebate into which the door rested was not a mere centimetre or two, but fully 7.5 centimetres on all four sides, ensuring it was near to impossible for the door to be forced with anything bar explosives.

Bufta appeared in the frame, his large body dominating the space. His face cracked into a big toothy grin as he recognised Arlon from his earlier visits. The conversations and learning that had occurred between them were mutually beneficial and enjoyable. The condition that normally prevented Arlon Grey from getting close to anyone failed to keep the irrepressible Bufta from enveloping him in a semi-constrictive bear hug that left Arlon gasping with the strength of the fellow.

With no further ado, Bufta, after re-engaging all the safety bolts, chains and padlocks on the door, led Arlon into his abode. A short tunnel sloping downward at a gentle angle brought them into the main living area, where threadbare furniture adorned the cosy space.

From within his tunic, Arlon hauled out the package he'd been carrying from his home: a large packet of his favourite coffee blend, which he handed to Bufta with a smile. The package was received gladly. A beaming Bufta raced into the next chamber to place a pot of coffee on the portable gas stove. Within moments, Arlon could detect the wonderful aroma of the blend circulating through the living quarters.

Once the coffee was consumed and they had caught up with each other's news, Arlon began to outline his plan.

CHAPTER TWENTY

Through a series of well-disguised sewage outlets, Arlon and Bufta made their way into the imposing biosphere, disabling the security monitors along the way. Bufta had been relegated to the lowliest of jobs to undertake for the elite rulers of the world: waste management. Once he had attracted all the wrong kind of attention for his stance against the actions taken by the rulers, his status declined sharply until he could descend no lower.

Bufta became an expert at navigating the labyrinth of pipes and tunnels beneath the dome, until he discovered the route that would finally allow him to escape. Only he needed to return every so often to stock up with fresh vegetables to survive. He would not eat the 'protein' bars, nor the algae of the feral humans. He found himself to be a pariah, totally on his own without the benefit of fitting into either society.

When Arlon had come across Bufta the first time, it was touch and go as to who might survive the encounter. Both combatants had certain advantages which they used with skill. Bufta was strong, large and deceptively fast, while Arlon had a martial arts background that made him particularly well-versed in most forms of defence and attack. They both realised swiftly that a stalemate would result from their conflict, and opted to hold a wary truce until they found a way to communicate with one another. A strong friendship developed over the weeks that followed.

Bufta only half understood the plan his friend outlined, getting mixed up with all the crazy talk of realities, dimensions and other Arlon Greys. The language barrier prevented him from fully comprehending the man. The only reason he agreed to the scheme, the parts he understood, was that it stopped the elite from doing something about invading those places his friend mentioned. Any chance to get even with the elite, Bufta would jump at.

Bufta knew of the area containing the highly experimental and dangerous laboratory where he suspected the time device to be housed. A series of super-shielded piping, carrying extremely hazardous and flammable material, all headed in one direction when Bufta first discovered them in his explorations of the biosphere's underworld.

The radiating gases and elements transported along the myriads of pipes had the potential to destroy the entire dome and its occupants if an accident occurred. Bufta became very concerned when he eventually perceived the extent of Arlon's plans. It was bold, audacious and extremely dangerous for everyone. Bufta's pivotal role in the plan worried him even more. Why he'd agreed to the insane scheme, he couldn't explain, other than it held a means of revenge. How he'd survive it, he couldn't say with any confidence.

After an hour of traipsing waist-deep through the foul detritus of the affluent elite rulers, Bufta led them out of the murk into a small antechamber. There they used the bottled water they'd carried with them to wash and change. They had opted to wade naked through the pipes, carrying their clothes and other essential items in an airtight container Arlon had strapped to his back. The stench was abominable. Had he not had a gas mask, the trek would have proven nearly impossible for Arlon. He couldn't imagine how Bufta had accomplished the task without one.

Arlon also donned his suit of Guardian armour, as he had taken to calling it, despite its ludicrous appearance. Bufta would not need one, as he would not be venturing too close to the laboratory, defended by a pair of sentinel Guardians, night and day. The sentries stood by an archway to a long tunnel that led to the only entrance into the laboratory. Once past the guards, Arlon would enter the laboratory, hope to subdue the scientists within, and force them to explain the procedures involved in utilising the time device.

CHAPTER TWENTY-ONE

Six years earlier...

Deep in the temperate rainforests of Victoria's rugged hinterland, on the eve of the winter's solstice, with crisp, white snowdrifts decorating the tips of the numerous mountains surrounding the area, in a ravine known to only a handful of locals, Hilda Haggerty led her small party down the length of her property.

With mere starlight penetrating the chilly darkness, Hilda hummed softly as she held out her hand with a morsel to tempt the local fauna out of hiding. Almost everyone watching recoiled at the grisly sight of the human eyeball she held.

Her exhalations formed small clouds of vapour in the still night air. The temperature was below freezing, as expected for that time of year in the Victorian forest of towering mountain ash.

She was the last Haggerty. The secret would have perished upon her deathbed, had Betty Payne not agreed to resume the ritual.

Not alone this time, in the dark, unafraid and highly attuned to her surroundings, Hilda waited patiently on her stump beside the permanent creek, listening to the gentle splash as the crystal-clear water washed against the many stones and boulders in its downward path. Much had occurred in the clearing of late, and Hilda held grave fears that her guest might not appear, might no longer be able to appear. She felt intensely sad about that possibility.

All that she did, everything she accomplished each year, was designed to follow through with the promise made to her father. She had continued the ritual he began in his youth, before she was born, before he met her mother. Her entire philosophy of life revolved around the anniversary of her birth, to continue the crucial act of reunification with nature.

Succumbing to lethargy and her ageing anatomy, Hilda blinked in an attempt to remain awake. Gradually her eyelids descended as gravity and age took their toll. Unable to remain awake for the first time since being introduced to the sacred tryst, Hilda nodded off, releasing the morsel she held in her hand to tempt the creature from its forest refuge.

Betty and Arlon stood behind Hilda Haggerty, supporting her ageing body. Tears came unbidden to Betty's eyes as she felt the last breath escape the old woman's lungs.

The morsel rolled from Hilda's wrinkled and liver-spotted hand on to the frosty grass at her feet. It continued for a metre down the slope before coming to rest against the base of another small tree stump.

Staring up blankly from its final resting place, the gelatinous globe remained there while the small troop vacated the clearing, believing the special event would not occur that year and, perhaps, never again. Alex and Arlon carried the lifeless form of Hilda Haggerty back up to the cottage, where they toasted her passing with mulled wine.

"Come with me, Mr Grey?" asked Betty.

"Where to?" he asked.

"Back out there," she explained.

"Why?"

"To witness the miracle, of course."

"Weren't we out there for that exact reason only moments ago?"

"No, we went out there with a wonderful woman to share her journey one last time. She always knew she wouldn't live long enough to see it happen again. She wanted me to take you all out there again so that I could sit on the stump in her place and reveal the miracle to you all. We are the caretakers of that magnificent privilege."

"It's getting very late for Tara to be up, Arlon. She can hardly keep her eyes open," said Clarice.

"What about it, kiddo? You up for it or not?"

"Arlon?" queried Clarice.

"Miss Grey is perfectly capable of knowing her mind. She'll

soon tell us if she's too tired."

"I want to go, Mummy," said Tara firmly.

"Uncle Alex and Aunty Dot?" enquired Betty.

"In for a penny, in for a pound, my dear. Lead the way if you think something will happen," said Dot with a warm smile.

Arlon faltered slightly as he passed through the doorway behind Clarice. He reached out automatically to brace himself and his hand found Clarice's shoulder.

"Arlon, are you okay?"

"Sure, just a momentary lapse. I need some sleep and a good holiday, I think. Why don't you go on ahead and I'll catch up in a minute?"

The small group left Arlon by the cottage as they trooped off down the path to the bottom of the property once more. Before Arlon could make a move to catch up with them, a hand appeared around the corner of the building, seizing Arlon by the shirt front. The hand hauled him back quickly without anyone noticing and before he'd had any thoughts about resisting.

What Arlon Grey saw, when he finally focussed on the figure belonging to the hand, stunned him to the core. He was face to face with his doppelganger, only dressed differently. Momentarily lost for words, Arlon watched in amazement as his mirror image placed a finger to his lips for him to remain quiet.

"Hello, Arlon," greeted the other man with his face.

It felt ridiculous to say the same thing back to him, so Arlon decided to remain quiet until he knew what was happening.

"This will be a bit difficult for you to accept, Arlon, but I would like you to trust me for a moment, knowing that I mean you no harm. In fact, I hope to help you in a significant way. I'm much like you, as you may have gathered. I don't just look, sound and act like you, though. I *am* you...in the future. Let's just call me Arlon B for the time being and I'll refer to you as Arlon A. Okay?"

Arlon A nodded his head uncertainly, still untrusting of the circumstances, contemplating that he might be dreaming or something.

"I've come from the future to save you and your family a great deal of heartache, Arlon A. That feeling you experienced just a moment ago that left you a little dizzy? That will get progressively worse very soon, with dire consequences. The energy in you has been awakened and strengthened after you used it. Without the knowledge of how to control it, you will succumb to its influence. The energy will take you on a journey to every corner of the known universe and beyond, following the path the asteroid took in reverse. I've come back to help you, to teach you how to control the energy."

"I'll play along with this strange dream. What happens if I don't accept your tutorial?"

"As I said, you vanish from this reality to follow the path of that meteorite. The one from Cid Island?"

"That doesn't sound so very devastating to me. I leave this reality for a while, so what?" asked Arlon A impatiently.

"Unbeknownst to you, your absence registers as six years in this reality, while you experience only six months away. Clarice, my...our...*your* wife...is heartbroken by your disappearance, and Tara grows up for a substantial part of her life without me...you, in it. I can change that for you...I hope," explained Arlon B.

"You hope?"

"I'm playing around with time paradoxes here and it's not a proven science yet. I'm doing my best to make it right but there aren't any guarantees."

"If I end up alive and well, which is supposedly proven by your presence here, then why should I bother with any of this?" asked Arlon A.

"For our family, Arlon, for our family is why you should be bothered with this. Clarice is the only person to have touched you romantically in your life and Tara is the only human ever to have tapped into your heart. To save them from being hurt, I will do anything, anything at all, including risking my life by coming here to an uncertain fate."

"Why would your fate be uncertain?"

"It's complicated."

"Uncomplicate it," demanded Arlon A.

Arlon B nodded and paused to collect his thoughts. "I've come back in time to change something in my past. If I succeed, and you remain here instead of disappearing, everything changes. That may include me winking out of existence altogether, or being stuck here, or any number of other possibilities. What I'm hoping to achieve is that you will remain here to continue your life with that woman down there, who loves you as no other person on this planet could, and that little girl who adores and admires you. She grows up into a fine young lady, by the way, just as you thought she would...only..."

"Only?"

"I don't want to give too much away. Then, again, it won't matter if I manage to change it. This is doing my head in. Tara devotes herself to finding you. She throws away what could have been an entirely wonderful life by pursuing her dream to become a detective like her father and find you."

"Oh, she's far too clever to want to do that."

"She would have been if you hadn't vanished in a few moments."

"This is real, then?"

"There's only one way I can prove that to you beyond a shadow of a doubt."

"And that is?"

"By revealing what you'll witness down there by that stump."

"Okay, go ahead."

"No, not yet. First I get to train you, then I give you the answer. Once you witness the miracle down there and confirm what I am about to reveal, you'll be armed with not only the proof of what I'm saying but the knowledge you'll require to resist the pull of that energy."

"How can you expect to teach me anything in a short time? I assume whatever is about to happen down there will occur soon?"

"Correct. Gosh, you have no idea how fulfilling it is to speak to someone of equal intelligence."

"Pretty sure I do...now. The answer?"

"What? Oh, yes, about the brevity of the tutorial? All I have to do is lay my hand on you to impart the knowledge, as you did to help Betty and Tara and that boy in the car."

"You know all that?"

"Of course I do. I did it all...six months...years ago."

Arlon A paused to reflect on the words of the man with his face and mind, claiming to be himself from the future. Allowing the man to place his hand upon him didn't seem like such a big thing for someone as proficient in martial arts as he was. He knew he would be able to defend himself if he thought he was in physical danger. He *had* experienced a momentary fade as he passed through the door before this man grabbed him. He *had* felt the tug from the energy within him, almost forcing him in on himself, as though it wanted to turn him inside out.

The thoughts warred within Arlon A while Arlon B stood by. Arlon B could see the conflicting thoughts parading through the mind of his former self, twisting the logic around, testing the parameters, stretching the limits until he came to an obvious conclusion. Arlon B needed to make it right, make amends for the intense hardship he'd caused his family. He only hoped that he was acting in the right vein.

Another thought entered his consciousness. If Arlon A didn't vanish and go through everything Arlon B had, then the knowledge of controlling the energy would not be forthcoming. In placing his hand on Arlon A to impart the control, it might only be a temporary measure, with Arlon A not needing to perfect it if he didn't require it any longer. Arlon A might escape leaving the current reality and Arlon B might be stuck in the past with him...forever! The past would affect the future. Arlon B would be the result of whatever happened to Arlon A, and the family he left behind in Arlon-the-scientist's home could be alone forever as well.

Of course, he could always be having a circular argument with himself...literally. He had to try it and hope that Arlon A would be wise enough to be convinced. He tried to place himself in the shoes of himself back then, which, for him, wasn't all that long ago. What would he have done if another Arlon had popped out of the blue with such a wild story? He couldn't say. It was just so far out of his comfort zone that he couldn't predict an outcome.

"Okay," said Arlon A suddenly. "I agree."

"Good man. I thought you might. More because you're curious to see if I can reveal the truth behind the supposed miracle down there?"

"Exactly," said Arlon A falteringly. It bothered him that someone could know his mind so well.

Arlon B leaned forward to place his hand on Arlon A's chest. The hand began to warm, with a glimmer of bluish light on the fingertips. The heat intensified, the glow increased and a tidal wave of energy flew through Arlon A, filling him with an intoxicating essence from his toes to his head. Arlon A observed and felt an immense amount of information and images flowing through him, flooding his mind. The searing heat from Arlon B's hand continued to burn its importance into the mind of the hapless recipient.

Arlon A flew through the voids, through the vast expanses of the universes, through the multitude of diverse realities. His mind was forced to observe and remember everything the other man had experienced: where he'd been, what he'd done. Without moving from his position, with the other man observing him, his hand pressed firmly against his chest, Arlon A was sent on a roller coaster ride of epic proportions, delivering him through one landscape, spacescape and reality after another.

Arlon B removed his hand from the other Arlon and stood back. That Arlon B didn't immediately vanish made him breathe more easily. He had yet to experience any diminishment of his memories or experiences, which meant that he might be safe from that particularly worrisome outcome. Arlon B could still feel the energy and sense the ability of control within him. So far, so good.

Arlon A staggered slightly, though he remained standing. The experience had disoriented and exhausted him. It took him several moments to regain his senses.

"What, what now?" asked Arlon A.

"Now you go join your family after I whisper in your ear," replied Arlon B. He whispered into the other's ear.

The surprise on the man's face after hearing the revelation made Arlon B smile uncharacteristically. He was ushered by the man around the corner, on to the path that would lead him to the bottom of the property to witness the miracle.

Arlon A joined the others at the bottom of the clearing. Betty asked everyone to stay behind while she sat on the stump. She bade them remain perfectly silent. The torches were turned off, leaving only the stars to cast their ethereal glow upon the small clearing.

Teeth were beginning to chatter noisily before a movement could be seen from the ferns on the other side of the creek. Peering every which way to ensure the area was clear of danger, the shy creature slunk through the icy waters of the creek to a distance of two metres from Betty, who was smiling fit to burst.

The mouths of those behind Betty opened in awe as the exotic creature glanced up at her with purpose. Its movements were slow and deliberate, indicating age. Arlon nodded his head appreciatively when he saw the creature's face clearly for the first time, then the distinctive stripes on its rump when the animal turned toward the lower stump where the eyeball rested. Gingerly, it made its way to the waiting morsel, which it picked up gently in its mouth. With one last look at the assembled audience, it swallowed the globe and made its way back across the creek to disappear in the fernery.

"It's a Tasmanian tiger!" shouted Tara suddenly, startling them all.

"Clever girl, Miss Tara Blaze-Grey. Yes, a thylacine. A carnivorous marsupial, which was believed to have been extirpated from the Australian mainland and New Guinea long before the last one was captured in Tasmania in 1930. Believed extinct, until now," explained Arlon in a voice that grew whisper quiet. "Damn! He was right."

"Did you just remember that?" asked Clarice without turning to him.

"No. I was told not so long ago by a very astute gentleman."

Just then the forest shone with a renewed twilight ambience, as if clouds that had been obscuring the stars had drifted past. Only, when Clarice turned, she saw that it was Arlon who was shining. He was enveloped in a halo of shimmering blue and white. He was trying to speak, but no words came out, and he was reaching toward her, toward Tara.

When Tara ran to him she clutched him tightly. Clarice watched as Arlon smiled at her, a smile so uncommon on Arlon Grey, a smile so welcome when it emerged on those rare occasions. He smiled knowingly, trustingly.

CHAPTER TWENTY-TWO

"Ar-lon? Are ok-ay?" asked Bufta in his halting English, when Arlon returned only moments after he had left.

"Yes, why?"

The two men walked back the way they had come, back to a section under the biosphere where pipes converged.

"Gone only like so," explained Bufta with a snap of his fingers.

"I don't think I could explain time jumping to you, mate. I did what I had to do. Now it's your turn. You think it will work?"

"Yes. Bufta make good show," said the big man, grinning from ear to ear and slapping his chest to indicate himself.

Arlon watched closely as Bufta went to work on the pipes he'd chosen for the task. He had marked them with bright blue chalk that glowed in the torchlight. Bufta raced down the tunnel a couple of metres to turn a valve off on one of the pipes.

"Nothing come now through here," he said, indicating the pipe on which he had turned the valve wheel. Using a blowtorch they had carried with them, Bufta placed the blue flame to the metal pipe to begin cutting.

"Are you sure there won't be anything coming through that pipe? Not even a little bit?"

"Bufta sure. Not little bit, not nothing."

After cutting through the pipe, he set aside the torch and raced down another branch of the tunnel to turn the valve off on another pipe. He cut through that pipe upon his return. A third pipe completed the cutting process. Two pipes from two directions were then welded onto the third single pipe that led towards the laboratory.

Arlon hung on to Bufta before he ran off to open the valves again.

"Explain it to me again. One pipe, this one, has what going through it?"

"Take stinky smell, gas, away from sewer."

"Methane, right? Methane gas?"

"Yes, stinky gas. Take away, make air good."

"And the other pipe has what?" asked Arlon.

The answer made no sense to Arlon. It was the language barrier. Bufta didn't know the word in English and Arlon had no idea what the other gas was in Bufta's language.

"Okay, never mind the name of it. How does it work?"

"Stinky gas meet other. Send in lab-or-atory. They mix with air and go boom."

"So the combination of the three gases is explosive?"

"Not knowing this, you say," admitted Bufta with a sad face.

"That's okay. I think I get the picture. More importantly, how long before...boom?"

"Bufta make boom."

"Yes, Bufta make boom. How long before boom, Bufta?"

"One!"

"One what? One second, one minute, one hour?"

"One!" he repeated enthusiastically.

"That's possibly cutting it fine, if your one means anything from a second to a minute. We'll have to time it perfectly. I can only hope the few hours I've had with you will let us do what I planned for us to escape the catastrophe about to be unleashed here."

"Bufta make boom. One!"

"Yes, yes, very good, Bufta."

It required Arlon on one of the valves and Bufta on the other to open them simultaneously. Then it was a race to meet each other at the confluence of the two tunnels. The disparate gases from the two pipes would combine at the new juncture, then only meet the other gas, commonly referred to as 'air', once it entered the laboratory. Arlon guessed that it would take very little time for the gas to travel the short distance to the lab. He had no idea how long it would take for the reaction to occur once the three gases combined.

He assumed that the reaction would cause the gases to heat up to a point of combustion. Arlon was unaware of the combination of gases that would require. His knowledge of chemicals was lacking somewhat. It was always possible that an unknown chemical element existed in the foreign reality Bufta called home.

Arlon and Bufta prepared themselves to activate their plan. They were a distance of some twenty metres apart and unable to see each other. Arlon shouted for Bufta to turn the valve. The second his valve was open far enough, Arlon sprinted to meet the oncoming man, wrapping him in a bear hug.

Down the corridor, from the direction of the laboratory, alarms were sounding, denoting the presence of foreign gases picked up by the monitors. Arlon hoped that an automated evacuation system had not been in place for such a contingency. If the gases were vented out of the lab before they had time to interact with one another, their plan was doomed to fail. He needn't have worried.

A loud explosion began only seconds before Arlon and Bufta were enveloped in a bluish-white halo. Lethal shards of metal and concrete assailed the pair before they vanished into the portal.

CHAPTER TWENTY-THREE

She had ventured outside for the first time since their arrival in the strange, yet familiar, world. Tara and Jarrah were playing a game inside when she left them to get some fresh air and explore their new yard.

It had been almost a day and a half since Arlon had left them to attempt to resolve the issues and save...everything. Naturally, she was worried he would either never return, or that the whole time-paradox thing would see them all vanish into nothingness. No matter how much Arlon explained his theory to her, she failed to be convinced about the outcomes he strived for. In truth, she was too confused to make any sense of it.

Clarice had seen her share of time travel movies and they always left her shaking her head. It shouldn't be possible in her understanding, didn't connect with her level of comprehension. She thought she'd known about all the spooky and weird stuff. The paranormal excited her. She had continued to surf the web each night in their own reality and enter the chatrooms to discuss all things outside the accepted norm. Most of it was rubbish, of course. It took a detective's mind to sort through the dross to locate and decipher the pearls of truth and wisdom hidden therein.

Arlon had convinced her to bring them all into the new reality, where a scientist named Arlon Grey lived in a seaside location similar to the one they'd left. Very little else was the same as the world they'd exited. The money was different, the people were different in subtle ways, according to Arlon. Clarice had yet to make contact with any of their neighbours or passers-by. Before she'd even had an opportunity to sample life in the new reality, Arlon was gone again.

Her heart had soared when he'd returned after all those years away. She'd seen the change and the joy in Tara as well. Then the bombshell he'd laid at her feet, about going back! That was when things became complicated for Clarice, when it seemed too much for her to cope. Uprooting herself and the children to travel by the most unconventional means in the history of the human race to another reality? How was Clarice supposed to accept that, if it were possible?

It had turned out to be possible. Arlon Grey had delivered on that score, just as she'd thought he might. Arlon Grey never made false declarations or impossible suggestions. At least, he never had. Clarice wasn't convinced about anything after he'd showed up. She suspected that she might not be dealing with the same man from her past at some point.

When she realised that it wasn't Arlon who had changed, but she, Clarice finally accepted his story. Arlon had been gone for only six months, while she'd had many years operating the business and raising children on her own. An intrinsic alteration to her priorities had occurred during that time. Her experiences had made her less reliant on anyone else, far more independent than before.

While Clarice had few regrets about her decision to follow Arlon into a new reality with her children, she experienced difficulty in attempting to convince herself that it was the right move. However, her choices were limited, according to Arlon. Stay where she was and end up fighting those monsters for the foreseeable future, possibly facing the masters once they figured out how to survive in another dimension, allowing Arlon to venture off without her on his solo quest? Or allow him to change the past and possibly remain where they were, with another Arlon Grey lurking in the background.

Clarice had to stop herself from going over all the possible ramifications of every decision. Her decision had been made and there was simply no going back on it, for better or worse, to be with her man and the adoptive father of her children. In the short time he'd been with Jarrah, the boy had shown a lifting of spirits. Not that the boy was morose or anything; he just seemed to light up upon seeing and interacting with Arlon. Clarice guessed that it might have something more to do with a general male bonding that any boy needs in his life, rather than a specific reaction to Arlon Grey. Not that Clarice would admit that to him.

For the day and a half since Arlon had gone off in that crazy bluish haze, Clarice had been mulling it all over in her troubled mind and confusing herself with all the possible conclusions. Despite every fibre in her body fearing any of the outcomes, she had never been happier and more content, knowing she belonged to him once more. Despite all her claims of independence and her lessons with Tara on that score, she smiled with the knowledge that she was in a relationship with the man of her dreams once more. Life had come full circle for her.

Clarice cried out in alarm. Arlon had appeared out of a shimmering portal beside her, covered in blood and supporting someone. Staggering forward, Arlon managed to straighten himself seconds before he face-planted into the dirt at Clarice's feet. She cried out anew when she saw flames on his trousers. Dashing madly to his side, she doused the flames with her torso up against his thigh, knowing how wrong it would be to pat the flames out with her bare hands, an instinctual reaction.

The man Arlon was supporting groaned in pain as he was laid on the dirt. He was bleeding profusely from a wound somewhere on his chest. Clarice watched as Arlon ripped open the stranger's rough tunic to reveal the site of the wound. A nasty chunk of sharp metal protruded from his chest.

"Arlon, are you bleeding?" asked Clarice in panic.

"I don't think so. Probably only minor lacerations if I am. It's Bufta who's going to need our help. Can you see if you can find some sort of first-aid kit in the house? I'll try to stem the bleeding if I can."

"Arlon? Who is he? Why don't you...you know? Do your thing?"

"After the exertion of getting us back here, I'm depleted,

Clarice. Hurry, I don't think we can afford to lose time on questions at the moment."

Clarice ran back through the rear door into the house. Arlon tore strips from Bufta's tunic to wrap around the shard in an attempt to stem the bleeding. He feared for any internal injuries the lethal-looking shard might have caused. Then there would be the greater fear of infection or tetanus derived from the rusty metal.

Bufta moaned as Arlon applied pressure around the wound. When he touched the metal, it burned his skin. Arlon decided that hot metal was a good thing. He wrapped some tunic strips around his hand to make another attempt at removing the shard. It came free with a sucking sound and Arlon could see that the site was semi-cauterised by the red-hot metal.

Clarice appeared with a small kit. He instructed her to fish out some antiseptic solution, washed the site with the stinging liquid, then proceeded to wrap a white bandage around Bufta's torso. The big man grimaced with the discomfort but held his mouth shut stoically.

Clarice and Arlon helped Bufta into the house, where he was laid on a sofa in the living room. Arlon noticed a breeze entering the room from a broken window pane, and the resulting wet carpet beneath. Although the storm seemed to have abated, the wet patch had not yet dried. A glance around the room told Arlon that little else seemed to have been damaged.

A glass of water was held out to the man by Clarice, who stood before them with questioning looks. Tara and Jarrah had entered the living room as well. Bufta opened his eyes to see a bunch of strangers and his friend staring at him. He started talking in his language, which no one but Arlon could understand.

"This is my family, Bufta. You're in my home in the other dimension. We made it. It worked. You need to rest up, though. You have a nasty gash where a piece of red-hot metal entered your chest. I don't think it punctured your lung, though. After I've had a chance to rest and eat a meal, I'll be able to heal that wound for you. Clarice,

Tara and Jarrah, this is my good friend, Bufta, from the world of the Guardians. He was one of the ruling elite before he was unceremoniously banished to the underworld of their biosphere to perform a menial and unpleasant task. Bufta, this is my family. Clarice, my wife. Tara and Jarrah, my adopted children."

"Your children, Daddy. Just your children," insisted Tara with a huge grin.

"Can I get you some more water, Mr...Bufta?" asked Clarice.

When he nodded uncertainly, Clarice returned to the kitchen to fill his glass. While she was there, she found a bottle of something a little stronger for the gent, thinking he might enjoy it more than water. She poured a generous two fingers of the amber spirit into a tumbler she retrieved from the cupboard overhead.

Bufta coughed when he sipped the liquid. Then a huge grin broke his kindly features. Surprisingly, Arlon indicated that he might like a wee dram of whisky as well, if that's what it was.

"Is that it, then, is it all over?" asked Clarice upon her return with Arlon's glass of alcohol.

"No, Clarice. Not yet. By destroying their time travelling device we may have curtailed their efforts to pursue us in the past. However, there are probably still Guardians present in other dimensions awaiting their masters to work out a method of joining them. They will have to be hunted down and...terminated. I cannot allow any dimension to have those things targeting the population while I have breath in my body. It was my fault, after all."

"Hold on. If you succeeded in preventing...you from vanishing that night in the forest, then you would never have turned up in that place to help a Guardian. That means they never found out about you or gained the ability to travel through dimensions. Right?"

"That is the theory, yes. But..."

"My brothers always said the only thing to follow a butt was shit."

"Very crude, Clarice. As I was saying, while the objective might have been achieved, Guardians were sent out to discover other habitable realities for the masters. I fear that they continue to exist in those dimensions even after everything I've done or undone. One glimmer of hope I have is that they did not retain the ability to move from one dimension to another, having lost that education by my reversal. They are effectively stranded where they ended up, with no way to return. Those outliers are the ones that need to be rounded up before they inflict too much harm."

"Are you trying to tell me that you're going to single-handedly take on the armies of Guardians out there in those other dimensions?"

"Not single-handedly," said Arlon, looking pointedly at them all in turn.

"Err...miss?" asked Bufta in a pleading voice, holding his empty glass up to Clarice for a refill.

"Do you think you should, in your condition?" asked Clarice kindly.

"Bufta make boom," he announced grandly.

"Clarice, you'll need to slow down your speech significantly when talking to Bufta. While he's made terrific progress with his English, he still has a long way to go before he's fluent, or can understand when someone speaks fast. Meanwhile, I believe he is very proud of the fact that he made an explosion in the masters' laboratory. He has been waiting quite a while to get back at the rulers for bringing about his fall from grace. Also, be aware that he won't eat any meat whatsoever after what he's experienced. He will never trust the source of any meat protein. Maybe one day I'll take him to an abattoir to show him what happens here."

"That will probably heighten his fears rather than allay them."

"Daddy?"

"Yes, Tara?"

"Does that mean you have to go away again, chasing the Guardians?"

"I'm afraid so. Fortunately, this reality doesn't have the time difference we experienced between our world and the other dimensions, so I should be able to make day trips, or perhaps a little longer. No different to before, really. I was always going off on trips here and there in my business. I have to do *something*, after all. We won't be desperate for money here but I still need something to occupy myself. I'm not quite as old as your mother, you realise? I'm still relatively young."

"Arlon Grey!"

"Ooh, you're in trouble now, Daddy. Never call a woman old, even if she is."

"Tara!"

"Are you going to help with the newly formed IDA, Clarice?"

"What's that?"

"I thought we could create another business here with the new name of the Interdimensional Detective Agency, or IDA, for short. Bizarre and mysterious just doesn't cut it anymore, does it?"

"I don't think so, Arlon. Someone has to look after the children. I want to devote most of my time to that endeavour. I thought you wanted to spend more time with them as well."

"I doubt I will be gone for extended periods, Clarice. Besides, I'll have Bufta trained up as my trusty assistant in no time at all. He'll be itching to get back at the masters. With him to help me I won't have to handle everything on my own, which will cut down on my time away considerably."

Clarice realised she hadn't refilled Bufta's glass for him and went into the kitchen to do so. When she returned, he had fallen asleep. The family watched as Arlon placed his hand on Bufta's chest. Though Clarice had witnessed the minor miracle before, it never ceased to amaze her.

"I thought you said you needed time to regain your energy levels?" asked Clarice with concern as she saw Arlon falter.

"You assumed he'd fallen asleep? He didn't. He fell unconscious from the loss of so much blood. If I don't do this now, he might not survive."

The Grey family watched in awe as the bluish glow continued

to intensify around Arlon's hand. Several moments later the light began to diminish and Arlon breathed a deep and weary sigh, catching himself from falling in a heap onto Bufta at the last moment.

EPILOGUE

Bufta regained his health in the following days while convalescing in a small spare bedroom. Each family member had spent some time with the likeable bear of a man, his broken and highly accented English causing no end of mirth for the children. Clarice grew very fond of him during their time together, reciprocated for the man.

Most pleasingly for Clarice over the following weeks that Arlon had decided to dedicate to his family, she had observed Arlon and Jarrah spending long periods together immersed in she knew not what. She only learned much later that it was secret men's stuff of the Gureng Gureng tribe, learned by Arlon during his time spent with Kami Bone, the boy's great-grandfather.

Arlon assumed that they would be unable to reunite the boy with his traditional family members in the new reality, and so had taken to studying the aboriginal culture intensely, to pass on those instructions for becoming a man of the tribe to his son. The boy grew more responsive and animated the longer the pair spent time together.

Jarrah was slowly finding his identity within his group of all-white family members. Though he was still very young, it had not escaped his immature notice that he differed greatly from his mother and sister, in more ways than merely skin colour. He loved them with all his little heart, yet it was insufficient to settle the feelings of disassociation he experienced. The patient teaching by the man, Arlon Grey, his new father, helped him immensely, offering him a sense of identity and belonging, an innate understanding of his heritage that he ardently lacked.

Arlon also spent many hours with his daughter. Tara became a new girl once she was reunited with her father. Though she never formally announced any changes, it seemed Tara no longer held aspirations of becoming a detective. Clarice knew that such a career path would not satisfy the woman she would eventually become in a reality where serious crime was almost unknown. It was truly joyous to watch her daughter blossoming into a woman without the constant and painful reminder that her father was missing.

Two other significant developments had Clarice grinning with hope and pleasure as she watched the interactions of the wonderful people in her life sharing a meal at the dining table.

During their time spent in the beach house owned by the scientist, Arlon Grey, a jovial man, apparently, it had become clear that her Arlon Grey did not measure up to their neighbours' expectations. This was a gross understatement in Clarice's understanding. Her Arlon Grey was as far from being jovial as it was possible to be.

Knowing that sooner or later suspicions would arise, Clarice had been making clandestine calls and arrangements over the phone and what passed as the internet. It had taken many hours of research, and countless more hours spent in consultations via video meetings, to achieve her goal without Arlon knowing. She stood at the table, tapping her glass with the handle of a spoon to gain everyone's attention.

"Thank you, I'd like to make a couple of announcements and a toast, if I may. So refill your glasses. Tara, you may have half a glass of wine, with some soda water added. Jarrah, just water, I'm afraid."

The group fell silent after charging their glasses. Bufta, impatient to resume his meal of roast beef, minus the beef and gravy, demurred, though with knife and fork raised in readiness.

"Let me start by saying how happy I am that we're all together for this Sunday lunch. I hope the roast was to everyone's liking?" Receiving enthusiastic nods from everyone, especially Bufta, Clarice proceeded. "As you know, our time here must end, as sad as that notion is to me and I'm sure to all of you. Too many neighbours have expressed concern over the odd behaviour and manner of Arlon Grey, whom they knew to be an extrovert and egregious, using that word in the archaic sense, and of a cheerful character. Before too long we will be forced to give explanations which we'll be hard-pressed to answer.

"We've all discussed many options about where we should base ourselves and still hold on to some semblance of our former lives. This is a strange reality for us, without any real connections remaining to us in a personal sense. If we managed to find our home in Indooroopilly, we would discover someone else living there, because the Arlon Grey from this reality, the scientist, did not venture away from his family home, where we sit today.

"So, after a ton of phone calls and online meetings with the help of the interpreting machine, I've found us a place to live that holds significance for Arlon and myself, and will possibly bring a measure of comfort to one other family member. On Friday, I signed the contract to purchase a property. It's situated around three and a half hours' drive roughly northwest of Brisbane. It will mark a new beginning for us all when we move there next week."

"Do you mean what I think you mean, Clarice?" asked Arlon.

"Yes, pretty sure I do. I bought the piece of land and the township we knew as Allies Creek. Although it has a vastly different name, we'll have come full circle, where it all started for us, Arlon. Tara, I know you only joined us after that particular episode, but I'm hoping you'll love it out there as much as we will. Jarrah, my darling boy, Allies Creek may not be somewhere you've experienced personally, and who knows if the cave with those Aboriginal paintings and artefacts exist in this reality, but I think you will find an affinity there, joining you spiritually with your ancestors and the land. In time, I hope you and Arlon can go on walkabout to initiate you into the tribe of your people, uniting your ancestors with ours."

When the general talk had subsided, all eyes returned to Clarice. "There is one other announcement I want to make. I would like us all to toast the newest member of our growing family," she said, placing a loving and protective hand on her abdomen.

The group devolved into wild cheers and tears as they rose to envelop Clarice in a group hug, including Bufta, who had no idea what was happening.

THE END

AUTHORS NOTE

It is with great sadness that I bring an end to the BAM Detective series. I will sincerely miss my characters whom I have lived with intimately since March of 2020. Every day since then, I have spent time with Arlon Grey and his associates, joining in their lives and experiences, feeling their frustrations and trembling with their fears. Parting ways with them leaves a hole in my world.

I have learned something quite significant about myself during the writing of this series, something that I should have realised many years ago. I can't be accused of quick thinking it seems, seeing as I'm over 60 now. Way back when calculators were first introduced to my life as a very young boy, I was shown a trick by someone, I forget who. If you press the zero button, followed by the decimal point, and then 7734 on a digital calculator. By turning the calculator upside down, the word hELL0 is seen.

I clearly remember looking at that and saying to myself that I could see a digital book like that in the future. I even had aspirations of inventing it. Unfortunately, I lacked the technical expertise to make it happen. Fortunately, I didn't make it happen at that time because I would have been about thirty years ahead of my time and very few people would have considered reading books on such a device back then.

The upshot of this anecdote is that I have discovered that I am either way behind the times in my thinking/writing, or way ahead of it. Just as Isaac Asimov can now be seen as being behind the times in a science-fiction writing sense, at the time he wrote his novels, he was way ahead of the general populace. I understand this to be what happened with this series. One way or the other; too far ahead of time or way behind, to be a profitable series.

I had hoped to make a 5-10 book series of it. That could only come to fruition if the books started paying for themselves to cover the costs of self-publishing and marketing. That hasn't happened, which has resulted in an end of the series for the foreseeable future. If by any quirk of fate the series gains significant traction in the future, I will attempt to rekindle the flames by beginning the spin-off series, The IDA(Interdimensional Detective Agency) series.

I would like to thank the readers who have supported my books and this series to this point. I truly hope they have entertained you as much as they have me. Bringing about the full circle of the story to end at Allies Creek, denotes the starting point for me as the author of the series. My inspiration for writing it sprang from my brief visit to the town of Allies Creek, purchased by my brother and sister-in-law.

The refurbishment of all 16 houses has now been completed, as well as parts of the arts and creativity centre. The big bar and reception centre will be next along with an amenities block for the small caravan park being planned. Well worth a visit if you are heading out that way soon.

ABOUT THE AUTHOR

Josef, born in Düsseldorf, Germany, immigrated to Australia with his parents in 1964. A near lifetime of creative pursuits has culminated in his desire to produce entertaining stories. Josef lives with his wife in the tiny outback town of Moulamein, NSW, Australia, where they own and manage a small caravan park, while they each indulge in their artistic endeavours.